Kensy and Max Books

Kensy and Max: Breaking News
Kensy and Max: Disappearing Act
Kensy and Max: Undercover
Kensy and Max: Out of Sight

Jacqueline Harvey

KENSY
AND MAX

=OUT OF SIGHT=

Kane Miller

A DIVISION OF EDC PUBLISHING

For Ian, Catriona and Holly,
who have almost moved mountains
to make this happen

Map of London

St. Pancras
Station

Regent's
Park

British
Library

FITZROVIA

British Museum

MAYFAIR

National
Portrait
Gallery

Serpentine
Gallery

Buckingham
Palace

Hyde
Park

St. James's
Park

Central London
Free School

Victoria &
Albert Museum

Victoria
Palace
Theatre

Natural History
Museum

KNIGHTSBRIDGE

Tate
Britain

The
Beacon
HQ

13 Ponsonby
Terrace

Map of
Paris

L'Arc de
Triomphe

Gare
du Nord

Grand
Palais

Musée
du Louvre

Centre
Pompidou

River Seine

Victoria's
Mansion

St Clotilde

Musée
d'Orsay

Tour
Eiffel

Les
Invalides

Musée
Rodin

Notre
Dame

CAST OF CHARACTERS

The Spencer-Grey household

Kensington Méribel Grey	Agent-in-training, 11-year-old twin to Maxim
Maxim Val d'Isère Grey	Agent-in-training, 11-year-old twin to Kensy
Anna Spencer	Dormant agent PA S2694, Kensy and Max's mother
Edward Spencer	Dormant agent PA S2658, Kensy and Max's father, son of Dame Spencer
Fitzgerald Williams	PA S2660, Kensy and Max's manny, Edward's first cousin
Song	PA U2613, butler

Central London Free School staff

Magoo MacGregor	Headmaster
Romilly Vanden Boom	Science teacher
Monty Reffell	History teacher
Willow Witherbee	English teacher
Elliot Frizzle	Art teacher
Lottie Ziegler	Mathematics teacher
Gordon Nutting	PE teacher
Theo Richardson	Drama teacher
Cilla Caspari	Librarian
Madame Verte	Languages teacher
Elva Trimm	Head dinner lady
Eric Lazenby	Custodian

Central London Free School students

Autumn Lee,	Kensy and Max's friends
Harper Ballantine,	
Carlos Rodriguez,	
Sachin Varma,	
Yasmina Ahmed,	
Dante Moretti,	
Inez Dufour,	
Misha Thornhill,	
Alfie Dingle	
Blair Braithwaite	New girl

Pharos

Dame Cordelia Spencer	Head of Pharos
Peter Petrovska	PA T113, editor-in-chief of the *Beacon*

Other

Victoria De la Vega	French actress
Harry Stokes	Investigative journalist at the *Beacon*
Jamila Assad	Investigative journalist at the *Beacon*
Trelise Fulton-Jennings	Social reporter at the *Beacon*

Case Note 18
Author: Fitzgerald Williams, Pharos Agent (PA) S2660
Subjects: Kensington Grey, PA A2713; Maxim Grey, PA A2714

Kensington and Maxim Grey were admitted as Pharos agents-in-training at the age of eleven years and one month.

FIELDWORK

Following an immediate threat to the twins' lives, which involved a bomb being detonated inside their London residence at 13 Ponsonby Terrace, Dame Spencer assigned Kensington, Maxim, Song and myself to keep watch on siblings Donovan and Ellery Chalmers in Sydney, Australia. Ostensibly, the mission was to secure the Chalmers children, after receiving intel that their mother, Tinsley, was planning to leave their father, Dash, and kidnap the children, taking them somewhere overseas. It was a well-timed operation, allowing the agency to investigate the London bomb plot and enable Kensington and Maxim to leave the city. Pharos has dedicated unlimited resources to solving this crime and, while progress has been slow, Dame Spencer is confident of an imminent breakthrough.

What initially appeared to be a simple surveillance exercise in Sydney became considerably more complicated as the children's new neighbor, Curtis Pepper, uncovered a plot by the headmaster of Wentworth Grammar School to employ two professional child singers to help his choir win the Sydney Choral Festival. The man was outed and his conspiracy foiled during the event at the Sydney Opera House.

Directly afterward, Maxim realized that several clues pointing to the where-abouts of their grandparents, medical scientists Hector and Marisol Clement, were erroneous and, while his parents and I were looking for them in Dalefield,

New Zealand, they were actually being held on a rural property called Dalefield in the Southern Highlands of New South Wales, near the village of Exeter. Maxim and his sister traveled by train to the property, although they were unknowingly followed by Curtis Pepper.

Upon their arrival at Dalefield, Kensington and Maxim located their missing grandparents in a bunker beneath a farm shed and set about freeing them. Dash Chalmers was already at the property, having been diverted there by his assistant, Lucy, who was working with Tinsley to ensure that she and the children could get away. Tinsley had received information regarding her husband's role in his sister Abigail's death many years beforehand, which proved the man's capacity for evildoing.

Twelve years earlier, Dash's henchmen kidnapped Hector and Marisol, staging their disappearance to look like an accidental fire in which they were both killed. At the time, the Clements were on the verge of patenting a cure for the common cold. They had been approached by Dash's parents, Faye and Conrad, owners of The Chalmers Corporation, one of the largest and most ethical pharmaceutical companies in the world, to propose a partnership. However, when Dash learned they were about to sign a deal to produce the vaccine, he decided the family business would stand to make far more money if he forced Hector and Marisol to create killer viruses that he would unleash on countries around the world, followed by their cures sold at exorbitant prices. None of this was known to Faye or Conrad, who believed their son to be an astute and clever businessman.

Dash's plan has made The Chalmers Corporation the richest pharmaceutical company in the world, bar none. His assistant knew he was selling vaccines at hugely inflated prices but had no idea he was holding Hector and Marisol hostage to create the diseases that required these cures.

While Kensington and Maxim freed their grandparents, Curtis Pepper managed to secure the latest round of viruses that were about to be released. Curtis is still unaware of the spy organization that the children belong to, but given his developing skills, there has been some discussion about inviting him into the fold, to join the agents-in-training program in London.

SKILLS, STRENGTHS AND VULNERABILITIES

The children have proven themselves worthy of their Pharos credentials on this mission, having rescued their grandparents and thwarted the release of further devastation caused by biological warfare. Their deductive skills, along with a willingness to take risks, has paid huge dividends. However, it would have been more sensible to include Song in their decision making this time. Maxim has displayed some impetuousness, which is uncharacteristic for him. Curiously, it was Kensy who questioned the logic in taking the train to Exeter by themselves.

TRAINING

Despite the change of scenery, the twins continued their combat training. Song has been acquainting them with the finer points of ninja stars and knife throwing, while I have focused on fitness and coding.

EMOTIONAL STATE

Prior to the bombing of 13 Ponsonby Terrace, Kensington had been distracted and sullen. She was encountering a few difficulties at school and was making a significant number of careless mistakes. She was also convinced that someone still had it out for her and Max, following a science experiment that was tampered with and caused a fire. However, following the bombing, Kensington seemed to bounce back very quickly both physically and emotionally. The "real mission" to Sydney improved her attitude greatly and, once it became apparent that there was more to the Chalmers children than met the eye, Kensington's focus was unrelenting. Maxim has largely proven steadfast and reliable throughout.

UPDATE ON THE DISAPPEARANCE OF ANNA AND EDWARD GREY

Anna and Edward continued communicating with the twins via Morse code through their watches and summoned me to join them in New Zealand. The family was reunited in Sydney and have now traveled back to the United Kingdom for a full debriefing and some important decisions about what comes next.

OTHER INFORMATION

Hector and Marisol Clement appear to have endured their twelve-year ordeal incredibly well, both physically and mentally. Further psychometric testing has been carried out in the United Kingdom, and they are currently staying at Alexandria, having learned the truth about Pharos. Cordelia has invited them to stay on and collaborate with Mim on her research, in addition to continuing their own work. For now, their existence is top secret as Dash Chalmers is still at large and considered highly dangerous. Rupert Spencer is on the man's trail and has not yet returned to the United Kingdom. The twins are overjoyed to be reunited with their parents and hopeful that they will continue their training at Central London Free School. They have also expressed a desire that Song continue to reside with us, as he is apparently a better baker than I am — a claim that is still up for debate.

CHAPTER 1

.... --- -- .

Anna Grey ran the brush through her daughter's unruly blonde locks, snagging it on yet another tangle.

"Ow!" Kensy yelped. "Mum, you know you can stop anytime you like."

Undeterred, Anna tugged at the knot, eventually wrenching it free. She frowned at the girl in the mirror. "Darling, you have such beautiful hair, if only you'd look after it at least a little bit."

"It's just hair, Mum – everyone has it," Kensy replied.

"Except Fitz," Max quipped as he walked into the room and sat down on the edge of the bathtub.

"True." Kensy chuckled. "Actually, I think I'd quite like to be bald. It would make life so much easier. No more washing and drying and brushing and styling."

Max and his mother grinned at one another.

"Are you talking about yourself?" Max said, dodging a swipe from his sister. "Because you hardly ever wash your hair and you definitely never dry it unless Fitz or Mum stands over you. As for the brushing and styling . . . um, bird's nest."

Kensy's mouth fell open. "Unlike you, who uses a bucket of product to make sure there's not a hair out of place." She rolled her eyes. "Let's face it, Max. Some of us are vain and some of us are not, and I know which category you fall into."

"That's quite enough, you two," Anna said. "It's been lovely having the past two weeks together with barely a cross word – let's not spoil it now, right before we're all faced with

2

the stresses of the real world again." She put the brush on the marble countertop and leaned down to give Kensy a hug.

"Thanks, Mum," Kensy replied, then stuck her tongue out at her brother.

The twins were excited about heading back to Central London Free School in the morning, although there was the small issue of their first Pharos review, which was taking place in a couple of weeks. It was Song who'd reminded them that they had better start preparing for it. He and Fitz had been dispatched to London from Alexandria too – to take care of the family, although Fitz was spending a lot of time out on mysterious business that he was not at liberty to discuss.

"Hello," Ed called from the entrance hall. "Anyone fancy a trot around the block?"

"Yes, please!" Kensy jumped up and charged off into her bedroom.

"Grab your coats and scarves," Anna called after her. She scraped her shoulder-length brunette hair into a ponytail and dug a tube of lip balm from her jeans pocket.

Max lingered behind for a moment. "Have you ever worn makeup, Mum?"

"Why do you ask?" She looked at the boy. "Do you think I need it?"

"No, of course not, but Granny Cordelia is always in full war paint and Grand-mère is never without lipstick and mascara," Max said. "I just thought maybe you'd like to."

Anna paused for a moment. "I used to. There was nothing I loved more than trying all the latest products. I remember there was a craze for matte lipsticks — I must have looked like a ghoul, but I thought it was very stylish at the time."

Max leaned against the door frame. "Why did you stop?"

"When life changed, I thought it was just easier to be me — even though I was doing my best not to be me at all, if you know what I mean. Now I'm out of the habit and I suppose I can't be bothered, although it would probably help. These dark circles aren't doing me any favors, are they?" Anna said, pulling at the skin under her eyes. "And I sense your grandmother thinks I should smarten up too."

"You're perfect just the way you are," Max said. "And it's entirely up to you whether you want to wear makeup or not. Don't let Granny boss you about."

Anna smiled. "You, my darling son, are as charming as your father." She kissed Max on the forehead. "Come on, we'd better get moving or Dad will think we've found something better to do."

Kensy was still going through the piles of clothes in the middle of her wardrobe floor, trying to find her scarf and beanie. Max disappeared into his room and grabbed a jacket from his walk-in closet while Anna trotted downstairs.

Ed looked at his wife adoringly, then wrapped his strong arms around her trim waist. "Good to be home?"

She nodded. "Gosh, I missed those kids."

"Ew, parent-kissing alert!" Kensy flew down the bannister rail, shielding her eyes. Max was right behind her and almost pushed her off the edge.

Anna and Ed chuckled as Kensy leapt to the floor and struck a gymnast's pose, as if she'd just finished a routine on the beam.

"Where are we going?" Max asked.

"For a walk along the river," Ed said, glancing at his watch. "We can't be too long, though, as you both need to get to bed. I thought it might be nice to get some fresh air and see parts of the old stomping ground under the cover of darkness."

Anna held her husband's hand. "We'll tell you some stories on the way."

Kensy and Max looked at each other.

"What stories?" Max asked as the twins followed their parents down to the kitchen and down again into the basement, where they got the new elevator. The group stepped inside and waited for the door to close before the unit began its descent into the earth. It came to a short stop, then hurtled sideways until it stopped and rose again. This time the door opened into a basement apartment in John Islip Street, which provided their current secret access route in and out of the much-expanded house.

"This is the weirdest elevator in the world," Kensy said, pondering the engineering required to power such a contraption.

"You haven't ridden in the one from your grandmother's office to Pharos HQ?" Ed asked.

Max frowned. "Nope."

"It's far more spectacular," Ed said.

"You'll have to show us," Kensy piped up. "Can we go now?"

Ed shook his head. "Sorry, that's up to Cordelia. I didn't get to see it until I'd left school."

Kensy pouted. "Not fair."

"Do you think we'll be able to use the front door again soon?" Max asked. "Not that I want to – this is much more fun."

"Well, it won't be until your grandmother decides that the scaffolding and plastic sheeting can come off the house, and I would think that might be a while yet," Ed said. "It was canny of her to buy up the whole street after the bombing. As knocking through to triple the size of this place would usually take much longer than it did, she doesn't want to arouse unnecessary suspicions. No one must know that we're living here for the time being."

It was impossible to see through the coverings from outside, although it did mean that the family felt as if they were living in a cave.

The group emerged onto the sidewalk.

"So what's this about a story?" Kensy asked as they rounded the corner toward the Thames. Kensy was holding her father's hand while Anna looped her arm through Max's.

"You know your father and I used to live here before you were born," Anna said.

Max's eyebrows shot up. "In Millbank?"

"At number thirteen Ponsonby Terrace, to be exact," Ed said.

"Is that why we've come back?" Kensy asked. "Because it was your old house."

"We did love it and it's nice to be somewhere familiar," Anna said. "And I'm going to enjoy my commute — my practice is being set up above the basement apartment in John Islip Street."

"Do you have to do any retraining, Mum? Given it's been so long and everyone thought you were dead?" Max said.

"I'll have to take some exams, but it's fortunate I have my records of service for the past eleven years," Anna replied. They turned left and walked past The Morpeth Arms before crossing the road to join the path along the river. Max couldn't help thinking the trees looked ghostly, their naked boughs swaying gently under the streetlights. "I kept up all my training – it was just under a different name – but I need to convince the authorities that I'm me. It's a curious situation to find oneself in."

"Of course!" Max said. "Your name isn't Grey at all. Neither is ours. We're Spencers. I can't believe I've never realized that before now."

Kensy turned to her mother. "Is Anna even your real name? Am I Kensington? Is he Maxim?" The panic was rising in her voice. Kensy didn't want to be anyone else. Life was weird enough without discovering that the name you had gone by for eleven years wasn't actually the one you were given at birth.

Ed drew Kensy closer to him. "Yes, your mother is Anna, I'm Edward and you two are

Kensy and Max. It's just our surname that changed from Spencer to Grey."

"Are we going back to Spencer then?" Max asked.

"What do you want to be called?" Anna said.

A small aluminum fishing boat with a noisy outboard motor zipped past on the river, followed by a sizeable cruiser. Several joggers dodged out of the family's way as well as a man walking a Great Dane.

"We could hyphenate," Kensy suggested. "Although I'm not sure if Kensington Grey-Spencer is quite right."

"Grey-Spencer?" Max wrinkled his nose.

"Sounds like dirty underwear." Ed chuckled. "Your mother and I are going back to Spencer, but we'll leave it up to you two to decide for yourselves. We completely understand that you've spent your whole lives as Grey, but there's no need to make up your minds now."

"Have you got any other surprises for us?" Kensy scampered ahead and spun around, walking backward and looking at her parents.

Anna frowned under the dim streetlight. "Like what?"

Max thought for a moment. "Were we adopted?"

"Don't be ridiculous — of course not," Anna said. "And I have the stretch marks to prove it. You know we never meant for any of this to happen. If we hadn't thought your grandparents had been murdered, we'd have raised you here in London. You would have always known Cordelia and Mim and the rest of the family. It's just that *I* couldn't bear the thought that you weren't safe."

The wail of a police siren sounded in the distance. Seconds later, the car with blue and red flashing lights roared past with another on its tail.

"We only left to protect you two," Ed added. "Your mother and I often wondered whether you'd hate us for it if the truth ever came out."

Kensy ran back and hugged her father. She looked up into his eyes. "Never. You were only doing what you thought was best."

"And, really, there aren't too many kids who've lived the life we've had. When you think about how much we've traveled and the places we've seen, we've packed a lot of experiences into eleven and a bit years. I wouldn't have changed it for anything and now we're starting a new adventure." Max grinned at his parents.

Ed squeezed his wife's hand. "Whatever did we do to deserve these two?"

"We must have done something right," Anna said, and turned to kiss her husband on the cheek.

But something on the river caught Max's eye. A speedboat was crashing across the wake of a river cruiser and heading straight toward them. It turned at the last minute and Max realized there was a passenger crouched behind the driver. He saw a glint of silver.

"Get down!" the boy yelled as a bullet whizzed over their heads.

Kensy hit the dirt and rolled away behind the nearest oak tree. Anna leapt in beside her while Ed grabbed Max and charged behind a concrete pillar.

The bullets kept on coming, though the gun obviously had a silencer attached since the noise was more like a *shooft* than a huge bang. Still, the sound sent a flock of starlings scattering out of the tree, behind which Kensy and her mother were hiding. Ed reached into the back of his trousers. Max's eyes widened as the man pulled out a .22-caliber pistol. He'd never seen his father hold a gun, let alone use one. With his back pressed hard against the pillar, Ed listened for the shots. When the firing stopped, he stepped out from his cover and took aim, but the boat's motor revved and the vessel powered away down the river.

Trembling, Kensy looked at her mother, who pulled her in for a fierce hug. "Oh, darling," Anna murmured into her hair.

Ed and Max ran over to them.

"Did anyone get a good look at the people on the boat?" Ed asked.

Kensy and Anna shook their heads.

"There was a name on the side," Max said hesitantly. "I saw it in the moonlight . . . *Deception.*"

Ed nodded, his face grim. "Great work, Max. I'll do a search as soon as we get back."

Max caught a glimpse of his mother's ashen face. "Are you okay, Mum?"

"I'm fine. I just didn't expect the deception to be on shore as well." Anna glanced at Ed. "I thought we weren't going back online."

Kensy had been wondering the same thing – if her father was helping Granny Cordelia run the newspaper, why would he need a gun?

"We'll talk about it at home. Come on," the man said, and gathered the family around him. Whoever had just attempted to kill them probably wouldn't try again anytime soon, but nothing was certain in this business.

CHAPTER 2

▪ ▬▪ ▪ ▬▬ ▪▪ ▪ ▪▪▪

"Goodness me, I cannot let you lot go anywhere by yourselves." Dame Cordelia Spencer sat the motorcycle helmet down on the end of the kitchen island. She ran her fingers through her gray hair and whipped a compact from her pocket, hastily reapplying her lipstick in the tiny mirror. "And, Song, where were you tonight? You should have been following them under the guise of taking Wellie and Mac for a walk. Is that really too much to ask? I've only just gotten everyone back and I don't want to be identifying you all at the morgue." She snapped the compact shut and perched on a stool, where the butler pushed a cup of tea toward her.

"It's chamomile, ma'am," Song said quietly, hoping it would soothe her jangled nerves. He'd already made a cup of the same for Anna, a strong brew for Edward and some hot chocolate for the children, though he hadn't mentioned he'd added magnesium and passionflower to help them all sleep.

Kensy eyed her grandmother's attire. Given the woman was dressed in black leather pants and a matching jacket, and carrying a helmet instead of a handbag, it would have appeared that she had arrived on a motorbike, but that didn't seem entirely likely. "Granny, how did you get here?" the girl asked.

A smile crept to Cordelia's lips. "On Carmelita. It felt good to blow off some steam."

"Carmelita?" Kensy prompted.

The woman took a sip of her tea. "Oh, I forgot you haven't met her yet. She's been away having some work done. She's my Ducati Monster, adopted sister to Esmerelda, who,

I might add, is looking very chic and sporty these days with her new chassis."

Esmerelda was the self-driving car who was teaching Kensy and Max to drive at Alexandria at Christmas. Unfortunately, something or someone caused her to go rogue, and the children were involved in a horrific fiery crash. They managed to escape unscathed, but Esmerelda required a complete rebuild.

"I'm glad Esmerelda is back together," Max said. "We've missed her."

"Just don't expect the old girl you once knew. She's changed and I'm not sure it's for the better," Cordelia replied, shaking her head. "I took her for a test drive the other week and, honestly, I think the technicians have given her a vain streak. The number of times she commented on her shiny body and sleek lines – she'll be asking for her own reality show any day now."

Everyone in the room grinned.

"Thanks for lifting the mood, Mum," Ed said.

The twins exchanged glances. "Where's Carmelita now?" Max said. Kensy was glad he asked. She couldn't wait to get her hands on the machine.

"Downstairs," Cordelia said, "but don't get any ideas. You two are not to touch her — ever — or at least until I change my mind. Now, to the business at hand. We need to find out who was trying to kill you tonight." The rest of the family were seated around the new island that Kensy had already decided was about the size of a small Pacific atoll.

Fitz thumped down the stairs into the kitchen. "I've done some research on that boat. It was reported stolen from Canary Wharf a few hours ago. The police have found it drifting near Kingston. The shooters left nothing on board and there's no footage of who took it, I'm afraid."

"Someone must have seen them," Ed said, setting down his cup. There was a steel edge to his voice and a look Kensy and Max had only ever seen once before — a couple of years ago, when they were living in Kaprun, Austria. A man had knocked on their door one evening and by the next morning they'd packed up and moved to Kitzbühel without so much as a goodbye to their friends. At the time, the twins were told their mother was desperately needed at the clinic there, but maybe that hadn't been the case at all.

"Our man at Scotland Yard said no one saw a thing and, thankfully, there have been no reports about the gunfire on the riverbank either, so it looks like they won't be launching an official investigation – at least not until a member of the public finds a bullet lodged in a tree tomorrow morning," Fitz said.

"You still haven't told us why you were carrying a gun, Dad," Max said.

"Precautionary measure," the man replied tightly.

"Well, I, for one, am pleased to hear it," Cordelia said.

Anna glared at her mother-in-law, who didn't miss the look on the woman's face.

"Whether *you* like it or not, you're back playing by *my* rules now," Cordelia snapped, and Anna blushed a deep shade of red.

Fitz looked at her, his features etched with concern. "We always knew there was the possibility that the past would catch up with us one day."

"What do you mean?" the twins demanded in unison.

"Everyone thinks you're dead – how would anyone know that you're back?" Kensy asked.

Song looked at Fitz, who turned to Ed, who glanced at his wife.

"Your father and Fitz upset some very bad people before we went off the grid," Anna said, eyeballing Cordelia. She was determined not to be cowed by her mother-in-law.

"But as far as we know, they've been languishing in a Russian prison for the past twelve years or so." Ed finished the last drops of his tea.

Fitz tilted his head to one side. "Why the Russians more than anyone else? We gave them all good reason to wage a vendetta. Remember Huang and his cronies, and Anders, and the Californian motorcycle gang?"

"There was Leroy and that horrid woman Lisbeth," Anna added. "I almost think she was the worst. Talk about an agent in sheep's clothing."

"She was dealt with for good, but what about the Colombians and that ghastly little toad Kapitis? Greek chap, thought he was Aristotle Onassis with none of his charm, wit or money as it turned out in the end," Cordelia said, her top lip curling involuntarily.

Kensy and Max looked at their parents in astonishment.

"I believe you are forgetting Delfroy and Kodiak," Song said, his eyebrows rising high on his forehead.

"Are you serious? Did Dad and Fitz offend the entire criminal underworld?" Kensy took a sip of her hot chocolate and glanced across at her brother. This news vastly lengthened the list of suspects who had been trying to kill the twins since they'd arrived in London. Apparently, it could have been anyone.

"So do you think the guys on the river were after Kensy and me, or you and Mum?" Max said, looking at his father.

Ed shrugged. "I really don't know." But one thing was for sure: he needed to find out before anyone was hurt – or worse.

Fitz scratched the top of his bald head. "I'll check the intelligence logs to see if any of our former friends have been active lately. As far as I know, Boris and his cronies are still guests of the Black Dolphin in Orenburg. They're all serving life sentences."

"Good." Cordelia nodded. "I can give you some additional resources."

Anna exhaled. "Anyway, as of tomorrow neither of you is going anywhere on your own. Not until we catch whoever was on that boat."

"But that's silly. We don't need chaperones," Kensy said. "We've had worse things happen before and we're agents too, you know."

"Agents-*in-training*," Cordelia corrected. "Since Fitz is taking up the investigation, your father is back on deck at the paper and your mother has exams to attend to, Song will not let you out of his sight – will he?" She glared at the butler.

"No, ma'am, not for one second," Song replied, glancing at the children. "I will let you go to the bathroom on your own," he mouthed.

Kensy snorted, though she was still smarting at the prospect of being babysat. She hoped the other agents-in-training wouldn't find out.

"This is no laughing matter," Cordelia said sternly.

When the family had been reunited at Alexandria just over a week ago, the atmosphere had been so light and happy. Now there was a horrible tension, especially between Anna and Cordelia. It made Kensy feel all churned up inside. Max was worried too.

"We'll agree, but only if Mum and Dad promise the same thing," Max said. "They need protection as well."

"Darling, that's not possible or practical," Anna replied. "And trust me, we'll be okay. Sadly, it's not our first rodeo."

Ed looked at his wife. "Oh really? Does that mean you've brought Bess out of the gun safe too?"

A smile played on Cordelia's lips. She'd make an agent out of that daughter-in-law of hers yet.

Anna sighed. "Well, if it's good for the goose . . ."

"That's settled then," Cordelia said. "Now, we need to discuss how we're going to tell the world that the three of you have returned from the dead and brought two eleven-year-olds with you."

Song offered more tea and passed around a plate of shortbread.

"What have you decided?" Ed asked. His mother had raised the issue at Alexandria last week and there had been a few options touted.

"I've lined up Evan Pinkstone. He believes he's getting the scoop of the century, but he doesn't know what it is yet. I think it's better to keep him in the dark until you arrive at the studio. The interview will be prerecorded on Saturday afternoon and will air on Sunday evening," Cordelia explained. "I've managed to do away with the live audience. It will just be the four of you with Evan. Fitz, I want you at the studio, but it's better that you remain off camera."

"Do you mean television, Granny?" Kensy was horrified by the thought.

Cordelia nodded. "Don't look so worried, dear. Evan will be working from a list of pre-approved questions, so nothing will come as a surprise. Plus, his show will be competing with the grand finales of some silly reality dance and cooking shows. Rest assured that we won't even make headline news in the morning."

Kensy wondered at her grandmother's certainty. While Cordelia could choose whether or not to run the story in the *Beacon*, she didn't control the rest of the media. "What if we say the wrong thing?" she asked.

"You won't. You and your brother will begin intensive media training tomorrow evening," Cordelia said.

Max gulped. "But we have to study for our first Pharos review."

"You'll be able to do that too," the woman replied. "You are Spencers, after all, and we're not prone to failure – in our business, that's akin to having a death wish." Cordelia smiled at the twins, but there was something in her gaze that sent a shiver down Max's spine.

Her words echoed in Kensy's head. No matter what, she and Max couldn't afford to fail.

"Anyway, I trust you've been enjoying the new space I had fitted out for you," Cordelia said.

"You mean the training room in the basement?" Max said. It was entirely dedicated to the twins' needs, equipped with a climbing wall, boxing ring, dojo, built-in boards for target practice, an ever-changing virtual parkour course and general fitness facilities.

"No, not that one," the woman said impatiently. She eyeballed Fitz and Song, making her displeasure known. "You haven't shown them yet?"

"We thought, as it was your idea, you might prefer to unveil it yourself," Song said. "And we have been very busy settling in."

Cordelia hopped down from the stool. "Come along then, children. This is rather exciting."

"May I come too?" Anna asked. She had

no idea what the woman was talking about either.

Cordelia nodded. "Of course," she said, and led them to the basement.

At the bottom of the stairs was the elevator that took them to the apartment on John Islip Street, and in front of it to the left was the door to the training room. Cordelia walked down a short corridor, which the children had thought was a bit of a strange dead end, and stood in front of a metal panel. She pressed her hand to the central plate, which began to glow white.

"Wow!" the twins chimed in unison.

"That's cool," Kensy gasped.

Cordelia was delighted by their reaction. "New technology – still being tested, but we decided to give it a go here and see what happened."

Anna rolled her eyes. "I don't see what's wrong with a good old-fashioned door lock myself."

Kensy frowned.

"Yes, I know, Kensy, I'm a luddite from way back," Anna said.

Kensy couldn't agree more. Her mother's mobile phone was practically Jurassic and she didn't believe in texting or social media. Sometimes she found it hard to believe they were related, given her love of all things technological.

The door swung open and overhead lights powered to life. The twins and Anna shielded their faces and squinted into the room as their eyes adjusted to the bright lights.

"It's a workshop and laboratory," Cordelia said. "Just for the two of you."

Kensy almost flipped at the built-in workbench with tiny trays of screws and other hardware, soldering irons and everything else she would need to work on her inventions. There was another section for woodworking and a separate glassed-off laboratory with cupboards full of scientific equipment.

Max hurried over to peruse the bookcase, which had a whole shelf dedicated to texts on coding, but it was the machine in the corner that really set his pulse racing. "Granny, is that what I think it is?"

"Sourced from Bletchley Park itself," she said proudly. "I thought you might be able to make some improvements."

"You did all this for us?" Kensy looked at the woman, a sheen in her green eyes.

"If you're going to become expert agents, you need somewhere to hone your skills," Cordelia replied.

Anna blanched. "That's only *if* you want to become agents. It's not an obligation."

"Of course not, dear." Cordelia smiled. "I would never force any of my children or grandchildren to stay in the family business against their will."

If she wasn't so peeved, Anna would have laughed.

"It's in our blood, Mum. It's who we are," Kensy said just as Ed, Fitz and Song walked into the room.

"Impressed?" Fitz asked.

"It's amazing," the boy gasped.

Fitz grinned. "Just don't blow up the house, okay?"

Kensy rolled her eyes. "Har-di-har."

"Excuse me, ma'am, but Sidney called and said to remind you that you have a very early meeting tomorrow," Song said. He held her motorbike helmet in one hand.

Cordelia checked her watch. "That's very thoughtful of him. I'll be off then."

The twins took turns hugging their grandmother tightly. "Thank you," Kensy whispered.

"My pleasure, darlings. And remember, I'm relying on the two of you – in so many ways," she said, her eyes meeting Anna's.

* * *

"What do you think about this television interview?" Max asked, perching on the side of Kensy's bed. He noticed the file their grandmother had supplied. It contained photographs and profiles of the staff at the *Beacon* who were also Pharos agents. There weren't as many as he'd thought there would be, but he was determined to commit them all to memory by the end of the week. Kensy was clearly doing the same.

His sister walked out of her bathroom, a toothbrush protruding from her mouth. "I hate it," she said, causing a river of toothpaste to dribble down her chin.

Max nodded. "Hopefully it will go the way Granny says and the press will leave us alone. It's a bizarre story whichever way you spin it. Someone is bound to think there's more to it, and the last thing we need is people sniffing around."

Kensy wrinkled her nose. "Do you think that Lisbeth woman Mum mentioned earlier was some kind of double agent?" This time she just managed to catch the dollop of saliva and paste that fell from her mouth.

"You're gross," Max said, shaking his head.

Kensy was gone for a few seconds and reemerged, wiping her face on her pajama sleeve. "Mum said she was an agent in sheep's clothing. I mean, if that's the case, we can't even trust people within Pharos."

"We know double agents are a thing," Max said. "Remember when Mrs. Vanden Boom was talking about that mole they discovered who'd managed to infiltrate the highest ranks and almost brought the organization to its knees?" He hopped up and inspected the textbook lying open on his sister's desk. "What are you studying?"

"Chemical compounds," Kensy replied, with a sigh. "And everything else."

"I know what you mean – I've been working on riddles. I bet there will be some doozies in the review." Max stretched and yawned, suddenly feeling the weight of the night's excitement bearing down on him. "Night, Kens. Don't stay up too late."

"I won't," Kensy said, catching his yawn.

She returned to her book as Max shuffled sleepily from the room. He wasn't planning to go to bed until he'd completed at least another hour of study. Kensy was banking on two.

CHAPTER 3

Autumn squealed and ran toward Kensy, almost barreling her over. "You're back!" she exclaimed, enveloping the girl in a bear hug.

"Steady on," Kensy said, but she was hugging Autumn just as tightly. "And yes, I'm very happy to see you too."

"Where's Max?" Autumn asked, glancing over Kensy's shoulder.

"Outside, being mobbed by Carlos and Dante. Anyone would have thought you guys were worried about us or something," Kensy said with a grin.

Autumn playfully punched her on the shoulder. "Of course we were."

There were lots of smiles and hellos on the way to their lockers and a couple of kids said they were sorry about what had happened. It took Kensy a second to register that they were talking about the "gas leak" at their house that had supposedly caused the explosion. The trainee agents thought they'd been in the hospital then recuperating at Alexandria – not conducting a mission in Sydney with the most unexpected of outcomes.

"Hey, Kensy! You look great," Alfie called.

Kensy stopped in her tracks and looked at him in horror.

The boy blushed a deep shade of red. "I mean you look really well. I'm glad you and Max have made a full recovery."

The girl felt a wave of relief. The last thing she needed after the unwanted attention of Van Chalmers in Sydney was another boy with a crush on her. She didn't have time for that. "Thanks," she mumbled, wondering exactly how much the trainee agents knew – by the sounds of it, their grandmother had contained the situation.

Kensy knelt down and opened her locker door. She was met with an avalanche of cards, which had been stuffed through the gap in the side. "Wow," she said, scooping up a handful. "That's so kind."

"See?" Autumn grinned. "It wasn't just me who was worried."

Kensy bundled the envelopes together to read later, then unpacked her bag and glanced at the timetable that was pasted to the inside of the door. She pulled out her English book and stood up. "Who's that?" she asked, gesturing to a tall man who was chatting to some of the senior boys. Broad shouldered, with a chiseled jaw and face full of designer stubble, he wore his dark jeans and black leather jacket with a casual ease. There was something familiar about him, but Kensy couldn't put her finger on it.

Autumn turned around to look. "Oh, that's Mr. Richardson, our new drama teacher. Isn't he dreamy?"

Kensy wrinkled her nose. That wasn't the word that had sprung to mind – there was something about the way he swaggered down the hall, laughing and high-fiving the kids, that didn't sit right with her. It was as if he was trying too hard. "Did he come to Alexandria for Christmas?"

Autumn's brown eyes widened. "Shush," the girl whispered. "And no, he didn't. He was hosting the *Holiday Variety Special* on television."

"Really? But I thought everyone who was part of, you know, was expected to be there –"

"Stop!" Autumn grabbed Kensy's arm and steered her toward the end of the hall.

"Why are we going this way?" Kensy asked.

"Because we have a lesson." Autumn frowned at Kensy. She wondered if the girl had forgotten how the school worked while she was away. "Are you sure it was just Max who took a hit to the head during the explosion?"

"Oops." Kensy grimaced. "I'm going to fail my first review, aren't I? There's just so much to remember and it doesn't help that it's not all straightforward."

"You won't be the only ones studying," Autumn said. "Magoo sprung a languages assessment on the rest of us while you were away – with a pass rate of ninety percent."

"What?!" Kensy spluttered. "Ninety percent? That's tough."

"Yours is worse – it's *ninety-five* percent for your first review," Autumn said. She could see the shock on her friend's face. "You didn't know that?"

Kensy gulped and shook her head. "What happens if we don't pass?"

"I'm not sure, but rumor has it there are punishments and training that amount to physical and mental torture – though that might just be something the teachers say to make sure that everyone gets through," Autumn said. "I only know of one kid who failed spectacularly, and he was never seen again."

Kensy inhaled sharply and made a mental note to share this information with Max.

Autumn glanced at the sign on the door of the girls' bathroom. The top half was old-fashioned opaque glass with the initials "WC" written in capital letters. At the moment they were black, and the girls needed them to be gold in order to get where they were going.

Kensy followed her friend inside, her stomach churning, and was surprised to find a girl crying at the sink. She had chestnut-colored hair pulled back into a low ponytail and was dabbing at her eyes with a tissue. The girl looked up and stared at them in the mirror. Autumn and Kensy glanced at one another before Autumn asked if she was okay.

"No," the girl sobbed, her bottom lip trembling. "I hate it here."

Kensy was almost certain she'd never seen her before. The girl had such striking violet eyes – not something easily forgotten. "Are you new?" Kensy asked.

The girl nodded. "We just moved a couple of weeks ago."

Autumn looked at her watch. If they didn't get her out of there soon, they'd be late for their first lesson and this morning it was all about mastering the art of the quick change. She'd been looking forward to it all weekend.

Kensy scouted the rest of the facility to see if any of the stalls were occupied, but there was no one else. She walked back to the sinks. They could always go the other way through the library, but that was sometimes trickier depending on how many students were about and what frame of mind Ms. Caspari, the librarian, was in.

A mouse of a woman, Cilla Caspari ran both the regular library and the Pharos one downstairs. Tiny and trim with gray hair cut into a stylish bob, Kensy had been startled to meet her when they arrived back at school after their trip to Rome. The woman had been away on leave when the twins first started. Apparently, Ms. Caspari had been at Alexandria for Christmas, but one of her skills was to make herself virtually invisible. Kensy thought she was quite mysterious and a bit prickly at times too.

"What's your name?" Autumn asked gently.

"Blair," the girl mumbled.

Out in the hallway, the bell rang loudly.

"What have you got first lesson?" Kensy asked.

"English with Witherbee the witch," Blair spat, her eyes darkening.

Kensy couldn't help thinking the girl had developed some strong opinions considering she'd just started at the school. Granted, Miss Witherbee wasn't her favorite teacher either, but she couldn't imagine what she'd done to deserve quite this much venom.

"Miss Witherbee's bark is worse than her bite," Autumn said, trying to coax Blair from her bad mood. "She's fine once you get to know her better."

"She hates me," Blair said.

"She hates *everyone*, and Autumn's right – she's not that bad," Kensy added. "Have you made any friends?" Kensy thought it wasn't likely if the girl had spent most of the time bawling in the bathroom since she'd arrived.

Blair shook her head. "It's so different to home."

"Where did you move from?" Kensy asked, though she had a feeling she already knew given the girl's accent.

"Australia," Blair said. "We used to live

in Sydney, where it was beautiful and sunny. London is so cold and grumpy and gray."

"Oh, I've just been . . ." Kensy started.

Autumn glared at her. "You really should get to class," she said meaningfully.

Kensy flushed at the realization of what she'd almost done. Seriously, what was wrong with her today? "Yeah, we're all going to be late," she mumbled.

"What are your names?" Blair asked.

Autumn smiled at her in the mirror. "I'm Autumn and this is Kensington."

Blair brightened a little. She turned on the tap and splashed some water on her face. Her eyes were puffy, but at least the tears had dried up.

Autumn passed her a paper towel, eager for the girl to hurry up.

"Maybe I'll see you at recess," Blair said as she headed for the door. They waited until it closed behind her then Kensy grabbed Autumn's hand and the pair flew into the last stall on the left-hand side.

"I was beginning to think she'd never leave." Kensy reached around the cistern and pressed the button. The back wall opened up and the pair scurried through into an elevator, which descended deep into the earth. Seconds later, the doors parted and they rushed along the subterranean corridor to their first class.

Meanwhile, Blair was still standing outside in the hallway. She was having second thoughts about going to English. If she feigned a headache, maybe the smiley lady in the office would call her mother to come and get her. She turned and looked at the bathroom door. Those girls were taking ages in the bathroom – and weren't they the ones who'd been worried about getting to class on time? Blair walked back inside. Oddly, there was no sign of either of them. She walked along the row of stalls, none of which were locked.

"Hello, is anyone here?" she called. "Autumn? Kensington?"

But she was met with stony silence.

Blair's brow furrowed. "Weird," she muttered, and walked back into the corridor. She looked up and spotted Mr. MacGregor, the headmaster, striding toward her.

"Oh, hello, Blair," he said with a broad grin. "How are you settling in?"

The girl gulped. "Okay," she whispered.

"Shouldn't you be in class?" the man asked.

Blair bit her lip. "I wasn't feeling well and I didn't realize the time. Miss Witherbee is going to kill me." A fat tear fell onto the top of her cheek.

"Are you all right now?" he asked.

Blair nodded weakly.

"Here, take this." Magoo pulled a pink card from inside his suit jacket and scribbled a few words. "Willow won't bark if she thinks we've been in a meeting."

"Thank you, sir," Blair said, taking it. She brushed at her eyes and then hurried down the hallway. As she reached the lockers, she turned to look back. Curiously, the man had vanished as well.

CHAPTER 4

Kensy was surprised to discover their lesson was to be led by the man she'd spotted in the hallway upstairs. Then again, all the staff at Central London Free School were agents as well as teachers. It was the students who were a mix of trainee agents and regular kids. A vital part of their training was to ensure that none of their civilian peers found out about what went on behind the scenes.

It was the same at the *Beacon*. Kensy had been studying the file containing the names and profiles of the Pharos-*Beacon* staff members. She had a feeling it would be part of their review to be able to name and identify the agents. So long as they hadn't changed their appearance recently, she felt reasonably confident.

"Nice of you to join us," the man boomed, as Kensy and Autumn slid into two spare desks in the back row.

"Sorry, sir," Autumn said. "We were helping a new student upstairs."

Theo Richardson ran his hand through his glossy dark hair and grinned. Kensy wondered if he'd ever done a toothpaste commercial, given his gleaming teeth. "You must be Kensington," he said. "I'm Mr. Richardson. Newly minted drama teacher and master of disguise – and world-famous actor, but you probably knew that already."

Kensy fought the urge to roll her eyes and gave a mumbled apology. The man's head was even bigger than she'd first thought. Max turned from where he was sitting in front of her, between Carlos and Dante. He beamed at Autumn, who blushed bright pink in response.

Theo Richardson looked to have a whole wardrobe of props positioned beside him. "Today, we're going to explore how to make a quick change – hence, an easy getaway – without drawing attention to oneself. Who can tell me some of the simple things you could do to alter your appearance?" A sea of hands shot into the air. The man pointed to Yasmina. "Yes?"

"Sunglasses and a hat," the girl answered. "And change the way you walk by shortening or lengthening your stride, or affect a limp."

"Perfect." The man picked up a baseball cap and grabbed a pair of dark glasses.

"They suit you, sir," Carlos said.

"It's not about my good looks, Carlos, though I'm sure you're right." Theo smirked. "This is about not getting caught. What if I wanted to pretend to be a woman? What would I use then?"

"A wig," Alfie called out.

"And a scarf, but it's going to be tricky if you're a hairy guy." Harper giggled.

"Why just guys?" Sachin objected. "My grandmother had the best moustache ever.

She said there was no point waxing because it grew back the next day."

"No, it didn't." Yasmina rolled her eyes. "You're making that up."

"Seriously, it did," Sachin protested. "My grandfather used to complain all the time that her facial hair was far more impressive than his."

"Which leads nicely to my next point – you need to think about the sorts of disguises that would work." Theo went on to demonstrate several quick-change techniques before he let the students loose on the costumes box. They had to work out how to change their appearance within five seconds and film the activity to see who was the most convincing.

Dante stuffed two pairs of socks down his top and wriggled his new chest into place, then threw on a dark, curly wig with a scarf over the top. Inez opted for a football jersey and a cap with her hair pulled up underneath, while Yasmina's transformation included a sun visor and a cane. Max donned a long blonde wig and tortoiseshell sunglasses.

"You look like Kensy," Carlos said to Max. "Actually, wait a second. I think you might be prettier."

"I heard that, Rodriguez," Kensy said, pulling on a tattoo sleeve, a purple mohawk and adding a fake nose ring.

It was all good fun until the teacher announced they were about to test their skills out in the real world.

"What do you mean, sir?" Dante said. The boy could have passed as an old nonna from behind, but he would never get away with it from the front, despite his new bosoms.

"Field trip, Moretti," the man said.

"But we've got classes upstairs next period," Autumn said. "Isn't it getting a bit late?" She had science and couldn't imagine Mrs. Vanden Boom would be impressed if half the class didn't turn up.

The man looked disappointed. "So, we can't just go out when we want to?"

"Um, no, sir, that's not really how school works," Dante said. "There are rules and paperwork, like risk assessments and stuff."

"Are you sure he's even a real teacher?" Max whispered to Carlos, who shrugged. It seemed a little odd that Mr. Richardson thought he could just take out the kids without consulting the other staff.

There was a knock at the door and Mr. MacGregor walked in.

"At ease, chaps," he said with a grin. He glanced around at the children. "I've always loved these lessons – they're so much fun. Oh, and good to see you back at school, Kensy."

"I'm not Kensy," Max replied. He absolutely could have passed for his twin sister.

"Well done, Max. I would never have known," Magoo said, and scanned the rest of the room. "Oh, now I see you, Kensy – that's a dreadful disguise. Your hair is a dead giveaway under that mohawk and that tattoo sleeve is loose – you wouldn't get away with that in the field."

Kensy's stomach twisted. She wished Mr. MacGregor would hurry up and leave. Max's attempt had been perfect and hers was a disaster.

"You'd better improve on that effort before your first review," the headmaster warned. "Trust me, you don't want to fail. The repercussions are truly *awful*."

Kensy didn't think she could have felt more embarrassed if she was standing there in her underwear.

Theo Richardson looked at the girl and gave her a reassuring smile. "We'll work on it," the man mouthed. "Now, what can we do for you, sir?"

"I came to see if we can make the announcement about the drama production at assembly," the man said. The pair then spoke in hushed tones before Magoo clapped his hands excitedly. "Brilliant! I can't wait. We haven't had a school play in a long while and I suspect there might be quite a bit of talent lurking about the place – oh, and if you need a cameo, you know where to find me. I used to be quite the artiste in my younger years." Mr. MacGregor fiddled about among the props. In a split second, his snowy hair was concealed beneath a skullcap, a chain of paper clips dangled from his left ear and there was a ring through his right eyebrow. He spun around dramatically. "What do you think, kids?"

The children burst out laughing. Anyone had to admit that, for a very quick change, the outfit was deceptively convincing despite the suit the man was wearing.

"I'll take that as a success – might go and try it out on Mrs. Potts," he said, and exited the room.

"What's all that about a play, sir?" Dante asked.

Mr. Richardson looked at the lad. "You'll hear about it this afternoon, and I hope to see some of you at the auditions."

"Which one is it?" Harper asked.

"*Romeo and Juliet*," the man replied.

"Shakespeare." Alfie pretended to gag. "Shoot me now."

"With a gangster twist," the teacher added. "I wrote the adaptation – and it's more of a comedy now than a romance."

"That sounds slightly better." Alfie wrinkled his nose. "So long as we don't have to do all that 'Romeo, Romeo, where for art thou Romeo?' I mean, why couldn't Juliet just say, 'Hey, Romeo, is that you down there?'"

The rest of the class laughed.

"I think you'll like this modern version," Theo said with an amused smile. "I can see you in the role of Mercutio – he hates pretension and you're probably about the right build for him too."

Alfie grinned. It wasn't often he was told his size was an advantage – except on the rugby field.

"I wonder if Max will audition," Autumn said with a sigh.

Kensy frowned at her. "He won't have time to be in the play. He'll be studying – like me."

Autumn's face fell. That was disappointing. Max would have made the perfect Romeo.

CHAPTER 5

"Hi, Song," Max said as he greeted the man outside the school gates. The boy leaned down to pat Wellie and Mac, who were dressed in matching Spencer tartan coats in aqua and tan. Since their return to England, there had been the odd few days with a promise of spring in the air, which Max loved, but he wished the season would hurry up and arrive properly.

"Good afternoon, children," Song said with a bow. "We have just returned from a very long walk – all the way to Battersea Park and back again."

"No wonder you two look so tired," Kensy said as she wrestled Wellie, who dropped to the ground and rolled onto his back with his feet in the air.

"What about me?" Song said. "I am exhausted and, unlike these two, I couldn't just plonk myself on the sidewalk and play dead. It is fortunate I had a pocket full of treats to coax them back home. I should have packed chocolate to motivate myself."

"I'd have given up too," Kensy whispered in Wellie's ear. She gave him another ruffle, then hopped up and brushed the grass off her skirt. The terrier flipped back onto his feet and gave himself a shake.

"So tell me all about your day," Song said as they set off toward home into a swirly headwind. "Did it live up to expectations?"

Kensy shrugged. "It was okay. Except that I have proven to be completely useless at the art of the quick change, which will no doubt be in our review."

"I remember it took me a long time to master that skill, but you are young and a good learner most of the time," Song said as they turned the corner. As Kensy and Max walked ahead, Song whipped a pair of sunglasses, a fake moustache and a beanie from his pocket and put them on.

"What have we got for afternoon tea, Song?" Max asked. His question was met with silence and he turned to ask again. "Kensy, did you see where Song went?"

The girl spun around. "Who's that with Wellie and Mac?" she said as the dogs rounded the corner. But it was Mac who gave the game away, when he caught sight of his master's altered appearance and yelped in surprise.

Max chuckled when he realized what the man had done. "Ha! Good one, Song."

To add to the effect, the man began to walk with a mincing gait.

"Very funny," Kensy said. "You know, you look like someone stuck a broomstick up your b–"

"Mum!" Max ran toward Anna, who was coming from the direction of the *Beacon*.

He caught up to her just before she was about to cross the road.

"Hello, sweetheart," Anna said, giving the boy a hug. "Did you have a good day?"

Max nodded. "We had a quiz on newspaper codes and I cracked every single one before anyone else in the class. Miss Ziegler said it was a record."

Kensy caught up to them. "I finished second and it was only by one minute."

Anna wrapped her free arm around the girl and gave her a squeeze. "I'm very proud of you both. Now, let's get inside. I could murder a cup of tea."

The family walked down to the basement apartment in John Islip Street. Song picked up a parcel from the doorstep. It was wrapped in brown paper with a giant black ribbon around it, addressed to Mr. and Mrs. Spencer. It looked to have been hand delivered.

"What's that?" Kensy asked.

"I suspect another gift for your parents," Song replied, turning the package over in his hands. "Word has spread throughout the organization of their miraculous return. We have a house full of flowers and more chocolate than the Cadbury's factory."

Anna took the parcel from Song. "We'll have to ask Cordelia to send a message – no more gifts. It's awfully kind but completely unnecessary."

Song pressed his thumb against the door lock. The mechanism whirred for a second before opening into the fully furnished basement apartment – except that nobody lived there. They walked down the hallway to the red door, where Song pressed his palm flat against the panel of glass in the upper half of the frame. It slid back to reveal the secret elevator. Their rollicking up-and-down ride took them directly to the basement of 13 Ponsonby Terrace in mere seconds.

The children charged up the stairs into the kitchen, which was almost three times the size of the old one. The beautiful white cabinetry had been designed around a central island that had already proven to be the most popular gathering place for the family – much more so than the four-hundred-year-old pine table that their grandmother boasted had been sourced from an abbey in Kent. While the house was undeniably beautiful, antique furniture wasn't the way to get the children's attention. But the row of freezer drawers in the butler's pantry was. Max had been looking for a plate when he stumbled upon them – six compartments containing just about every flavor of ice cream known to man. He and Kensy had agreed to work their way through the entire selection over the coming weeks, which pleased Song, as many of them were his own recipes and he was keen to know their thoughts. He had long been contemplating a side hustle running an ice cream store – if only there were more hours in the day. Adjacent to the kitchen was a vast family room with a comfy sectional sofa and multifunction television screen that linked directly to their grandmother's office.

Fitz was sitting at the kitchen table, reading the afternoon edition of the *Beacon*. "Hello," he said, looking up and rubbing his tickly nose before returning his attention to the paper.

There was a chorus of greetings from the children, Song and Anna. Max took off his coat and hung it up, then placed his bag on the rack beneath it, digging out his math book. Kensy flung her bag into the corner and let her coat drop to the floor, much to the chagrin of her mother and Song. The butler was about to pick it up when Anna shook her head and raised her eyebrow at her daughter.

Kensy sighed. She scooped up her coat and threw it at one of the hooks, landing it perfectly. Then she did the same with her bag, which clattered onto the rack below. "Better?"

Song nodded. "Your aim is very precise, Miss Kensington. Well done."

Anna placed the brown paper package on the table along with a handful of shopping bags.

"What did you buy, Mum?" Kensy asked, hurrying over to investigate.

"Some lovely new clothes for work." Anna pulled out a beige shirt along with an equally drab sweater. She held them up triumphantly. "What do you think?"

Song grimaced from where he had just put the kettle on. To avoid revealing his true opinion, Max buried his head in his homework. Kensy burst out laughing.

"You can't be serious, Mum," she protested. "They're horrible. And *brown*. Even I know that's a color reserved for Franciscan nuns and old-man cardigans. You should take Song with you next time you go shopping. He's got style."

The man blushed. "I would be honored, Mrs. Spencer. And we will need to find something for you to wear to Lady Adelaide's book launch next week too."

"What book launch?" Anna prayed Cordelia wasn't planning to trot the family out to her friends' social soirees like some sort of circus act.

"I will let Dame Spencer tell you about that herself," Song said, and retreated into the butler's pantry.

"Well, hopefully my other parcels are more successful than the clothes, which are clearly a disaster," Anna said glumly as she pulled out two books. "Max, darling, this one's for you," she said, placing a thick atlas on the table in front of the boy, who was already halfway through his algebra homework.

Max's face lit up as he opened the book to the first page. "Mum, this is awesome! It's got the lot – every town and village in the whole world must be mapped in here."

Kensy rolled her eyes and feigned a yawn.

"Perhaps you'll like this better," Anna said, handing the girl a book on miniature mechanical engineering.

"Whoa!" Kensy snatched it up. "You know, I've got another insect just about ready for its test flight – it's a butterfly, but there are a couple of things I can't work out. Between this book and Dad, I'll have it up and running in no time." Kensy had been shocked to learn that it was their father who had designed and built the watches that had been their primary communication devices when their parents had been missing. He'd been keeping those skills quiet forever, but now that she knew, Kensy was keen to get his help with her own inventions.

"I'm glad some of my shopping was a success, even if they are old-fashioned books with no interactive intelligence." Anna grinned and wandered over to the island, where Song had made her a cup of tea and cut a slice of carrot cake.

"And you have date night to look forward to as well," Fitz said.

Anna frowned. "Date night?"

"Ed called earlier and said to tell you that he's made a reservation at The Morpeth Arms for seven o'clock," Fitz said. "He tried your phone but couldn't get through."

Anna dug it out of her handbag and realized she'd missed three calls. She'd had it on silent when she went for her meetings and forgot to flick it back. She hated the phone at the best of times.

"Are we going too?" Kensy asked. "I love The Spying Room – it seems so corny now that we know the truth, but it's still fun to see if you can spot the MI6 agents across the river, doing whatever it is that they do."

Fitz shook his head. "Media training begins tonight, and I believe you have a review to start studying for as soon as you've finished your afternoon tea. Anyway, I haven't managed to ask you yet – how was your first day?"

"Good," Max said, sliding onto a stool at the island. "We had quick-change lessons this morning with our new drama teacher, Mr. Richardson, and they announced the school is putting on a play for the first time in years. It's a modern take on *Romeo and Juliet*."

"Theo Richardson?" Fitz said brightly.

Kensy nodded and rolled her eyes. "He who loves himself to death."

"I remember, as a lad, he always wanted to go into the theater. He's made quite a success of it," Fitz said. "Impressive young man."

"Oh, he's gorgeous," Anna said. She held up the sweater and wondered if it was really as bad as the others had said. "I wonder why he's teaching now."

Kensy wrenched open the fridge door. She took out a carton of milk, then fetched a tin of chocolate powder from the butler's pantry.

"I don't see what's wrong with him," Max said, getting a glass and spoon out too.

Kensy made a face. "He's so . . . full of himself."

"Perhaps he's just confident," Anna said.

"*Over*confident, more like," Kensy scoffed, heaping twelve teaspoons of chocolate into her glass before she looked up and spotted the frown on Song's face. She pushed the tin toward her brother, who stopped at six.

"Divas aside, are you going to try out for the play?" Fitz asked.

"We don't have time for thespian endeavors," Kensy replied, licking her spoon. "Not if we're going to pass our reviews."

"Oh, that's a pity, darling. It would be nice to have another cultural experience after your choral efforts in Sydney." Anna smiled. "And I love *Romeo and Juliet*. I played Juliet myself in high school."

"You never told us that," Kensy said. Come to think of it, there was still so much about their parents' lives the twins knew nothing of.

"The review will be over in a couple of weeks," Fitz said. "Besides, acting is a big part of the spy business. You could at least go to the auditions and test your skills. It might help with your media training too."

"I'm in," Max said, swizzling his spoon

around in the glass of chocolate milk.

"Autumn will be so pleased," Kensy quipped, ignoring her brother's withering glare.

Anna looked up at her son. "Do you like her, Max?"

"Yeah, she's nice," the boy replied.

"She wants to be Max's girlfriend," Kensy teased.

"That's not true," the boy retorted. "We're just friends. Like Carlos is *your* friend."

"Okay, you two, break it up," Fitz said. "You'd better get your homework done. We'll start media training after dinner."

"Are you doing it?" Kensy asked. She hadn't known what to expect when her grandmother told them about it last night.

Fitz rolled up the newspaper and pretended it was a microphone. "I've always enjoyed the idea of being a hard-hitting journalist. Tell me, Kensington Grey, what did you know about your parents' lives – who they were before you and your brother were born?"

The girl rolled her eyes. "Duh, clearly nothing."

Max grimaced. "I don't think that's the

way to endear yourself to the audience, Kens."

"What would you know?" she huffed, and stuck her tongue out at him.

Fitz nodded, not giving anything away. "And what are you looking forward to, now that you're back in England and reunited with the rest of your family?"

"Weekends and holidays at Granny's mansion, Alexandria," Kensy said, feeling pleased with herself. This whole interviewing business was rather easy.

"Did you have any idea that you were on the run your whole life?" Fitz pressed, switching tack. "The rumor mill is swirling with claims that this has been one big attention-grabbing stunt by Dame Spencer, to drum up interest in the ailing *Beacon*."

"Of course not!" Kensy snapped. "And there's nothing ailing about the *Beacon*. Sales are fine. Granny has really gotten on board with all that online stuff – she's a modern businesswoman."

"O-kay." Fitz exhaled. "We have some work to do. They're probably not the ideal responses."

Kensy threw her hands in the air. "Great. So I'm hopeless at talking to the media as well as quick change," she moped.

"Don't worry, sweetheart," Anna said. "That's why Fitz and Song are going to give you some training — so you're prepared for anything. Although, if I know your grandmother, she will have everything under control."

Max looked at Fitz. "What *did* you do before you all disappeared? I've been meaning to ask you that for ages."

Song chuckled.

Kensy arched an eyebrow. "Was Fitz an accountant or something?"

"Not quite," Fitz replied with a wry smile.

"Well, come on, don't keep us in suspense," Max said.

"Fitz was actually an actuary," Anna revealed. "One of the brightest brains in the country. He's much smarter than your father and me."

"Speak for yourself," Ed quipped as he reached the top of the stairs from the basement.

"Sounds dead boring to me," Kensy said.

"You're not wrong," Fitz agreed. "It was far more of a challenge looking after you two."

Song chuckled and threw some diced onion and garlic into a pan as Anna greeted her husband and told him about her shopping disaster. Max showed Fitz his algebra homework and Kensy fed some leftover cake to Wellie and Mac under the counter, all the while stewing about her disastrous day.

* * *

Kensy lay back on her bed and adjusted the earpiece. She would have felt guilty for eavesdropping on her parents' private conversations if it wasn't for their track record of disappearing and attracting multiple attempts on their lives. This was the only way she could rest easy, and it wasn't like she did it all the time. She closed her eyes and listened.

On the way to the pub, her parents talked about their day, which almost sent Kensy straight to sleep. They'd been greeted by a chatty waitress with a strong northern accent and, not long afterward, ordered their food.

"I'm sorry about the other night," her father whispered.

"Me too," Anna replied. "But to be honest, I'm scared, Ed, and I'm tired of feeling that way."

Kensy was surprised to hear it – her mother was always so stoic.

A long silence ensued. Kensy began fiddling with her earpiece and yawning.

"Mushroom risotto," a waitress announced cheerfully. Kensy heard the plate land on the table with a thud. "Steak, medium rare, sir." She must have been more careful this time.

"Thank you," Ed said. "Excuse me, have we met before?"

"N-no, I don't think so. Sorry," the waitress replied.

"What's your name?" Ed asked, and Kensy stiffened. She wondered if this woman was one of those enemies with a vendetta. The problem was that it didn't have to be the criminals themselves; it could be their family, their friends, their underlings – just about anyone.

"Eleanor . . . Rigby, from Liverpool," the waitress replied. "Enjoy your meals."

The woman was either a terrible liar or her parents were die-hard Beatles fans. She knew it was the name of one of their songs, as Fitz adored them and she even caught Song playing the *Yellow Submarine* album recently instead of his usual twangy country ballads.

"So should we eat or not?" Anna said. Kensy detected a note of concern in her mother's voice.

There were sounds of fumbling followed by Ed saying "cheese."

Kensy smiled when she realized that they must have been pretending to take photos of their food, when in reality they were checking their meals for traces of poison or interference with an app on her father's phone, which he'd shown the twins the other night. It had just been developed.

"All clear," he said.

"Sorry. I guess I'm feeling paranoid after the . . . incident," her mother said.

Kensy winced as her ears filled with a thunderous chewing noise and she hastily turned down the volume. This device was even more powerful than she'd expected, given it was in her mother's pocket.

"Why don't you come and work for Mother?" Ed asked. "You know that's what she wants."

"She has plenty of resources already and it's bad enough she has my parents now and the children – and you, even though you're going to deny it."

"Of course I'm working for her – at the newspaper," Ed replied.

Anna sighed. "I'm going back to my own practice, Ed, whether your mother likes it or not."

Kensy wondered if her father was telling the truth. He had been carrying a gun, after all, and it was clear her mother thought he was back in the game. Knowing now how she and Max felt about the family business, she was certain the call of Pharos would be too hard for her father to ignore.

CHAPTER 6

Carlos slid into the seat beside Max, his brown eyes wide. "I can't *believe* you two didn't tell us that someone shot at you the other night – and from a speedboat! On the *Thames*!" he whispered in outrage. The boy shook his head and opened his carton of flavored milk. "Wow, my life is so depressingly dull."

"I'll swap anytime," Kensy said, looking up with a deadpan expression on her face.

"As if," Carlos scoffed. "My entire existence is comprised of school, homework, school, more homework, studying Spanish – which, by the way, everyone thinks I already know, but I actually don't. I grew up speaking English like the rest of you, so I'm completely set up for failure. I swear I'm a child mouse on a hamster wheel."

Autumn giggled. "Your whiskers are less twitchy."

Sachin thudded his plate on the table and sat down beside her. "Who's got whiskers?"

"Carlos was just telling us about his sad existence," Max said.

Sachin wrinkled his nose. "Oh yeah, I wouldn't want to be him. His life is so boring, unlike yours." He popped a potato chip into his mouth and grinned. "So who's trying to kill you guys this week?"

"No idea, but hopefully we'll find out before they succeed," Max said.

The dining hall was full of chattering children and the smell of sausages. Elva Trimm had served up bangers and mash with thick gravy and green beans followed by bread-and-butter pudding with custard for dessert. Unlike many English schools, whose gymnasiums doubled as their lunchrooms, Central London Free had the luxury of a dedicated dining space, so at least it didn't have to be set up and dismantled each day. Portraits of past heads of school gazed down from the walls along with honor rolls containing the names of head prefects, duxes and house captains. There were lists of sports champions too. Kensy was aiming to have her name up there somewhere by the time she was in Upper Sixth. She'd only just realized that Fitz had been dux of the school and her father had been the head boy. So maybe what her mother said about Fitz being the smartest was true after all.

"We should lay a trap using you two as bait," Sachin said, waving his fork in the air. Unfortunately, he got a little too carried away, flinging a piece of sausage over his shoulder. It thwacked Misha in the side of the face.

"Hey!" The girl stood up and turned around. "Who did that?"

Sachin cowered behind Autumn, although she didn't exactly provide cover considering he was a head taller than her.

Autumn rolled her eyes at the boy. "Wimp."

Misha picked up the errant sausage and threw it at Sachin, who caught it with the skill of a seasoned fielder.

"And as for a trap," Autumn added, "that could possibly be the very best idea I've ever heard . . . for getting Max and Kensy killed."

The proud grin on Sachin's face dissolved. "Aw, come on, Autumn," he scoffed. "We're playing for keeps in this game and we have a moral responsibility to look after our own. If someone is trying to kill Kensy and Max, we should take them out first."

The children began talking over the top of one another, debating the merits of the idea, their discussion getting louder and more animated by the second . . . until Blair appeared at the end of their table with her tray in hand.

"Can I sit down?" the girl asked. Without waiting for a reply, she shuffled in next to Carlos.

For a minute, no one said a thing as they concentrated on their lunches.

"What?" Blair asked.

Max made a mental note to ask for more training on how to handle awkward situations without looking completely silly. "Hi," he said, and introduced himself.

"Everyone, this is Blair," Autumn said. "She's new. Just started a couple of weeks ago. She's from sunny Sydney and isn't a fan of English weather to date."

There was a cacophony of hellos around the table.

"Don't expect it to change anytime soon," Sachin said. "I would much rather live in sunny India, except it's a bit crowded where my family comes from."

"How was your English lesson with Miss Witherbee yesterday?" Autumn asked.

"Fine," Blair said, nibbling on a chip. "You were right about her bark being worse than her bite. She said I should try out for a part in the play."

"That's great," Autumn said. "Picking up an extracurricular activity is the best way to find your feet."

Blair smiled and threw her chestnut tresses over her shoulder. There was something about the way she did it that riled Kensy.

"You know yesterday when we met," Blair said to Kensy and Autumn before she took a bite of her lunch. The girls looked at her and nodded. "Where did you go afterward?" she asked, stabbing a piece of sausage.

"To class," Kensy said.

"No, I mean, how did you get out of the bathroom? I walked back in to ask you something and you weren't there and I didn't see you come out," Blair said.

Carlos, Max and Sachin traded wry grins. Their entrance to the Pharos training area was located in the boys' bathroom and they'd had their fair share of close calls – one involving Graham Churchill, who saw Carlos disappear through the back of the wall. Fortunately, Sachin had entered the bathroom after Carlos and spotted the kid standing there with his jaw gaping. He spent the next thirty seconds convincing Graham that Carlos was actually an aspiring magician. It was pure good luck that Carlos had forgotten something he needed for his lesson. He reappeared just as quickly as he'd gone and Graham believed their explanation. Although the boy did spend the next six months badgering Carlos to teach him card tricks and sleight of hand.

"Oh, you must have been looking the other way down the hall," Autumn said, as smooth as silk. "We saw you when we were leaving."

"But I was standing right outside the door," Blair insisted. "I'm not wrong."

"Yeah, we did," Kensy said. "You were so upset – maybe you didn't realize or forgot."

Blair's forehead puckered, but before she could argue further, Max spotted Mr. Richardson at the end of the room with a tub full of what looked like scripts in his arms. "Hey, Blair, didn't you say you wanted to audition?" he asked.

Blair looked up and saw the man, who was talking to a spotty kid she recognized from her English class.

"You should go and get a script," Kensy said with an encouraging smile, hoping that would get rid of the girl once and for all.

Blair slipped out of her seat. Trouble was, she collected a wad of pages and headed straight back to them. "I got scripts for everyone," she said, and sat back down, passing them around the table.

"Which part are you trying out for then?" Kensy asked the girl.

"Juliet, of course," Blair said, as if getting the role was a foregone conclusion.

"Good for you – that's ambitious," Autumn said. She'd done some research last night and decided that, if she was going to audition, it would be for a much lesser part.

"I think you'll be up against Misha," Carlos said. "And she's the most naturally talented actress I've ever met."

Kensy and Autumn both suppressed the urge to smile. A truer word was never spoken, given that the poor girl had spent years on an undercover mission, forced to cozy up to the nastiest girl in the school. Misha should have been awarded a BAFTA for her performance. Now that that particular assignment was over, she was pretending to see a counselor to get help for her bullying ways – just so none of the regular students wondered how she could undergo such a miraculous change of character.

"Who's Misha?" Blair asked, her eyes narrowing.

"The best actress in the school," Kensy said. She glanced at her watch. They had a lesson downstairs with Mrs. Vanden Boom straight after lunch, and Kensy was keen to get there early to ask her about some of the chemical compounds she'd been studying for her review. She nudged Autumn's leg. Thankfully, the girl was tuned in. "See you all later," Kensy said as she stood up, and Autumn followed suit. "We've got to see Miss Ziegler about some homework before the bell."

The girls cleared away their plates and collected their books from their lockers, then headed to the girls' bathroom at the end of the corridor. Kensy double-checked that the sign on the door was gold before slipping inside. Autumn pushed open the last stall door on the left and the two of them scurried through. Kensy reached around and pressed the button

and the wall slid back. The girls disappeared –
little did they know there was someone else
there too, watching their every move.

CHAPTER 7

— —. .. —. — .—. .—. — —.. . .—

Kensy and Autumn hopped out of the elevator and walked along the concrete corridor to the Pharos science laboratory, where Mrs. Vanden Boom was about to take them through the basics of explosive materials. As it was part of their training, Kensy felt a little less uneasy than usual. It wasn't so long ago that a regular science experiment had led to her accidentally setting fire to the lab upstairs. They'd never gotten to the bottom of who had replaced the baking soda with powdered magnesium and, although Granny said they were making progress, they still didn't know for sure who had planted the bomb which destroyed 13 Ponsonby Terrace either. Along with the gunman in the boat the other night, the list of potential killers was really beginning to add up.

The children jostled each other as they picked up safety glasses and lab coats on their way in the door, the noise levels rising.

"Hurry along, everyone," Romilly urged. "We've got a lot to get through this afternoon."

The room was not dissimilar to the labs upstairs in the main part of the school – except for the concrete-reinforced walls, three-inch-thick metal doors, blast-proof glass cases and bomb-disposal robots roaming about. It was also at least three times the size, with areas set aside for all manner of scientific endeavors, including mechanical engineering, robotics, biological research and quantum physics.

A row of containers sat on the lab bench in the front.

"Please find a seat and make sure you pay close attention as there will be a quiz at the end of the lesson," Romilly said to a chorus of groans. She pulled on a long pair of double-thickness latex gloves and lowered her safety glasses from the top of her head to cover her eyes. She started with magnesium, which she placed into a toughened glass box, then reached through the two-way hatch and lit the fuse.

It sizzled before the flame exploded, causing a bright flash. Romilly talked the children through the reaction and why it behaved the way it did. But it wasn't just the explosion that was creating interest.

Inez nudged Harper, who took a moment to comprehend what she was getting at. When she finally did, the girl recoiled in horror. Harper then caught Kensy's eye and motioned toward the door. Kensy frowned, wondering if she had food stuck between her teeth, then almost fell off her stool when she realized what was going on.

"Autumn," she whispered, poking her friend in the ribs.

"Ow!" Autumn protested.

"Goodness me, girls, whatever is the matter?" Mrs. Vanden Boom clicked off the taper she was holding and closed the box in which she had been about to detonate a stick of gelignite. She glanced toward the door. "Oh dear."

By now all eyes were on the girl.

"What is this place?" Blair asked. She gazed around at the floor-to-ceiling glass cabinets filled with curiosities. Several rows of shelves contained scientific equipment, the likes of which she'd never seen before, while there was a whole section of dead animals preserved in jars of formaldehyde. She hadn't yet glimpsed the huge terrarium housing Leo, their resident anaconda, at the back of the room. In one corner there was a stripped-down chassis of a car and a motor scooter too, which the children had been learning to hot-wire. "Why didn't anyone bring me here on the school tour, and how come you have to get into the elevator through the back of a bathroom stall? That doesn't seem very hygienic."

Romilly smiled. "Hello, Blair. Please, come in and sit down."

The rest of the children wondered what the

teacher was playing at. Blair wasn't supposed to be here. No one outside of Pharos was meant to access the underground. It was the highest breach of security, yet the woman was practically inviting the intruder for tea and cookies.

"But why are you all down here? And is that TNT?" Blair asked, looking at the shatterproof glass box on the bench. "Isn't that dangerous? Why would we be using stuff like that in school experiments?"

The students looked at one another.

"Max, would you mind sliding over to the next stool?" Romilly said. "Blair can sit between you and Carlos. Take a seat right there, dear."

Max did as he was bid, still unsure as to why Mrs. Vanden Boom was being so accommodating. He pondered the idea that she might have triggered a silent alarm, sending a troop of Pharos agents into the room to cart Blair off to some safe house, never to be seen again. But no one came.

"I'd like you all to make some notes about the materials we've tested thus far," Romilly continued, as if nothing remotely strange was happening at all. Her instruction was met by a sea of blank faces. "Chop chop," she said. "We haven't got all day."

That would mean showing Blair another part of Pharos the children weren't allowed to remove from downstairs – their virtual thought-pads, which were called Upton Sinclairs and which recorded both notes and thoughts. They were tricky gadgets, especially if the teacher caught a glimpse and those thoughts hadn't been particularly favorable about the lesson or the teacher. There was also a stylus to be able to write on the tablet just as one would in a regular notebook – sometimes this was safer.

"But, Mrs. Vanden Boom, are you sure about that?" Dante said, a quiver in his voice.

"Absolutely," Romilly answered. "If you don't record the experiment soon, you'll forget. There's a pop quiz at the end of the lesson, remember."

"But I never got to see the experiment at all," Blair complained. "You'll have to do it again. I don't understand what's going on."

"I'll be over to help you in a second, dear," Romilly said, and quickly scurried to the storeroom.

"Why is she being so nice to her?" Kensy whispered to Autumn. "Vanden Boom never calls anyone 'dear.'"

Blair looked around at the unusual mix of students. "Is this like an advanced class or something?" she asked. "You're not all in the same year, are you?"

"Yes, that's it," Max said. "Special class for science nerds."

"Well, that's definitely not me," Blair said, and jumped down off the stool. "My class must be back upstairs. And this place is weird. Is that a *snake* back there?"

Max leapt off his stool and blocked her path. "Actually, I'm sure . . . you're meant to be here. Right, Carlos?"

Carlos nodded, ready to pounce if the girl made any further moves to leave.

Mrs. Vanden Boom trotted out of the storeroom and headed straight for Blair. "Sit down, dear. Have you worked out how to use your Upton Sinclair yet?"

"No, it's blank," the girl replied. Although, if she'd looked carefully, there was a whole paragraph outlining exactly what she was thinking – including that Max was the cutest boy she'd ever seen. "How . . .?"

Romilly leaned in close to the girl and pulled something from the pocket of her lab coat. Then, with lightning-fast reflexes, she placed the gadget against Blair's neck. In less than a second, she was out cold. "Hold her," Romilly instructed Carlos and Max.

The boys lunged forward to prevent the girl from hitting the floor. Romilly cradled Blair in her arms while Alfie hurried over to help. Together, he and Max and their teacher laid Blair across one of the benches.

Romilly was shaking her head. "Goodness me, how on earth did she find her way down here?"

Autumn and Kensy grimaced at one another. "That's a big fat fail for my review," Kensy whispered.

"What did you do, Mrs. Vanden Boom?" Dante asked. "Did you have to kill her?"

There were some nervous giggles around the room.

"Dear me, Moretti, we're not in the business of murdering curious children at Pharos. It's a memory-erasing serum. Blair won't remember a thing that's happened in the past hour. We'll take her up to Mr. MacGregor's office and through to the sick bay and she can sleep it off. She'll wake up with a bit of a headache, but she'll be as right as rain . . . I think."

"So, this has happened before?" Yasmina asked.

"Not often, thankfully, but yes — and we had to figure out a way to deal with it," Romilly said. "This is a potent concoction, but we have found that the timing can be a little off. Needs more work, really."

"So, you can erase people's memories?" Kensy said. It sounded dangerous and awful but, on the other hand, quite useful too. She would have liked to get her hands on the formula.

Romilly nodded. "Yes, but we need to find out how Blair got down here and make sure that it doesn't happen again."

Autumn reluctantly raised her hand. "I think she followed me and Kensy."

The girl explained what had happened yesterday and how they'd assumed Blair had gone to class, but apparently she'd gone back inside to look for them.

Romilly sighed. "Thank you for being honest, girls. It's much better we know the truth. I hope you've learned your lesson because you must *never* let it happen again. If Dame Spencer finds out, I can't guarantee what she will do about it. The last trainee agent who let in a civilian spent a month in isolation studying famous speeches in history, which he then had to recite word for word before being allowed back into the program."

The woman fetched a gurney from the storeroom – the sort you'd find inside the back of an ambulance. Kensy had never been into that room, but it seemed like a veritable treasure trove.

"Boys, could you help me, please?" she said to Alfie and Max, who lifted Blair onto the contraption.

Blair groaned, startling the class. Her eyes opened then closed almost immediately and she began to snore.

"Is she all right?" Kensy asked.

"Oh yes, the serum has a few side effects, but I think she'll be fine. I'll check her over with the RUOK 2.0 once we're upstairs. I'm afraid our lesson's going to be cut short. I suggest you all make your way to the library and study up on everything there is to know about explosive substances," the woman said. "Pop quiz will have to wait until next time."

"Do you need a hand?" Max asked Mrs. Vanden Boom.

"Actually, that would be great," the woman said. "This thing is not the easiest to negotiate around corners and I don't want to tip her off – it's always hard to explain the bruises."

Romilly watched the children leave before she and Max guided the gurney out into the corridor. She used her thumbprint to lock the door. It wouldn't do to have any more curious incidents, especially as she'd left several explosives out on the bench, knowing they had a closing window of time to get Blair upstairs.

They pushed the contraption to the end of the hall and then entered an elevator which Max had never ridden in before. He was surprised when the doors opened to a narrow corridor he didn't know existed.

Romilly had phoned ahead to let Mrs. Potts know they were on their way. The woman let them into the headmaster's office from the corridor and explained that Magoo was out for the rest of the day. Max could almost feel the sunbeams that radiated from Mrs. Potts's face. Dressed in another of her handmade creations, Daphne's sweater had a family of alpacas stitched onto the front and she wore a mismatched pair of black and white Scottie dog earrings.

She peered at the sleeping girl, who was now snoring gently. "Oh dear, I had a feeling this one was trouble. Before her interview, she pouted and panted like a dying trout in the reception area, then turned on the charm when Magoo arrived. Her parents seemed eternally grateful when they were told we had a spot for her, as if perhaps they'd been refused other places. Anyway, take your time, Romilly – make sure that she's tip-top. And let's hope she wakes up before the bell." Daphne smiled and hurried back to her post.

"Right," Romilly said, whipping the RUOK 2.0 from her deep pocket. She pulled the cover from the end and set it on the desk, then projected a virtual image of the girl with all her vital signs into the space in front of them.

Max was observing intently when he glanced down at Blair. "Uh, Mrs. Vanden Boom," he whispered urgently, "I think she's awake."

Blair's eyes were wide open and she began to speak, but it was all nonsense – like several languages mixed together.

"Don't worry, that's just her brain recalibrating," Romilly said.

Suddenly, the girl expelled a loud burst of wind. It sounded like a balloon exploding, followed by another and another. Finally, the girl gave a long belching burp that ended in a high-pitched pop.

"And that?" Max giggled.

"Was something she ate." Romilly chuckled, then swiftly turned a peaky shade of green. "Goodness me, were there eggs at lunchtime?"

Max shook his head. "Sausages and mash."

"She clearly has a sensitive stomach, poor girl." Romilly checked the data and decided that, apart from her tummy upset, Blair was in fine shape. "Now, let's move her into the sick bay and hope she wakes up soon," the teacher said.

Max looked around the room, wondering where Mrs. Vanden Boom meant for them to go.

"Oh sorry, Max. If you head over to the bookcase in the corner, you'll find a door to a secret passageway that leads to the sick bay," the woman said. "Third book on the second shelf from the left."

Max quickly located the tome. He reached up and pulled it toward him, but unlike the other times he'd used a concealed pivot door, there was no resistance and the book clattered to the floor.

"Oops, I meant the fourth book," Romilly apologized. Blair let out a little grunt followed by a groan and a wheeze and another pop. "Hurry, please. I think she might be starting to wake up."

Max crouched down and grabbed the book from the floor. *The Struggles of Leadership* – it seemed like something Mr. MacGregor would read. The boy could only imagine that it was a constant struggle keeping a whole school full of staff and students in check. There was a piece of paper sticking out from the side. He opened the page to stuff it back in, but when he noticed his and Kensy's names written on the top, he paused to take a closer look. The rest of the text was in code, which he thought slightly odd.

"Max!" Romilly urged.

The boy hesitated, then stuffed the paper into his trouser pocket. Kensy would have done the same – actually, Kensy wouldn't have even thought about it. He put the book back on the shelf before he pulled on the fourth one, releasing the latch. The door opened and, seconds later, he and Mrs. Vanden Boom had steered the gurney down a hallway and into the back of the sick bay. They transferred Blair to one of the beds then left the girl with Mrs. Potts, who was on hand with a glass of water and a warm washcloth for her forehead.

Max returned to the library downstairs, where it seemed Ms. Caspari had commenced a reign of terror. He'd never seen his friends so quiet before and no one was game to mention what had happened earlier. Carlos attempted to ask Max how everything had gone, but the woman had silenced him with a raised palm.

When the class was finally dismissed, the children hurried up to their lockers. "Sorry, got to go," Autumn said to Kensy, packing her bag at lightning pace. "Dentist."

Kensy stood up and spotted Mr. Nutting, their PE teacher, striding down the hall, resplendent in his red-and-navy tracksuit and sneakers.

"Ah, Kensy, just the person I was hoping to see," he said with a grin. "I wanted to mention that, if you'd like to do any extra training before you know what, I'm happy to spend some time with you and Max. I know you've had a rough time of it and I'd like to see you do well."

"Thank you, Mr. Nutting," Kensy said, surprised by the offer. "That's really kind. Maybe tomorrow afternoon? We'd just have to let Song know we'll be finishing later."

The man nodded. "Tomorrow afternoon it is."

Kensy stood up and smiled to herself. Perhaps the other teachers would be agreeable to some extra training too. It couldn't hurt to ask, and she could certainly pay them in chocolate – the pantry was full of it.

"Meet you outside," she said to Max, who was talking to Carlos in hushed tones. She skipped down the front steps and saw Blair standing at the gate, staring skyward. The girl looked as if she was in some kind of trance.

Max hurried out and stood beside his sister, scanning the road for Song, who was on approach with Wellie and Mac. The twins walked toward the exit.

Kensy nudged her brother. "Do you think she's okay?"

Max shrugged. "How are you feeling, Blair?"

At first, the girl didn't respond. Then she wrinkled her brow, as if she didn't quite understand what he was asking. Perhaps the memory-erasing serum had some other side effects Mrs. Vanden Boom didn't know about. Kensy wondered if she should let Mrs. Potts know Blair still wasn't quite right.

But in the blink of an eye, she turned and smiled at Kensy. "I'm great, thanks. See you tomorrow and don't forget to learn your lines," she said, then bounded down the street toward the Tate Gallery, as if nothing had happened at all.

CHAPTER 8

━━━━━━━━━━
━━━━━━━━━━

▪━▪▪ ▪▪ ▪▪▪ ━ ▪ ━▪

━▪━▪ ▪ ▪━▪▪ ━━━ ▪▪▪ ▪ ▪━▪▪ ━▪━━

Max sat at his desk and opened his seventh codebook of the evening. He'd plundered the library in the workshop downstairs as soon as they got home and dragged every possible authority he could find to his room. The books were now scattered all around him, but, despite spending the last three hours hunting through them, he'd found nothing remotely resembling the gobbledygook on the page he'd taken from Magoo's office.

He sat back against the chair and yawned widely, then took off his glasses and rubbed his tired eyes. Perhaps that was it, Max thought suddenly. He sat up straight again. The code might only be meant for two people – the writer and the recipient – which made it near impossible to decipher. Why the headmaster had a whole page of coded information about him and Kensy hidden inside a book was a complete mystery and one he was determined to solve.

He placed the paper inside the notebook and returned it to his bookshelf when a loud bang came from downstairs. Max leapt out of his seat, his heart thudding in his chest, and raced to the door. He rushed down two flights of stairs to the kitchen. Song was already halfway to the basement.

"Don't worry!" came a muffled yell. "Everything's under control!"

Max breathed a sigh of relief and wiped the sweat that had collected on his brow. Kensy and her crazy inventions again.

"I swear your sister will be the death of us all," Song said, and trudged back into the kitchen.

Max grinned and nodded.

"Here, have a scone. It will settle your nerves, Master Maxim," Song said, nodding at the plate of freshly cooked treats on the island. He picked one up and took a bite.

"Thanks, Song." Max did the same and went to see what near disaster had been averted this time. He opened the door to the workshop and ducked, narrowly avoiding being hit in the head by Kensy's latest drone. It was the butterfly, which she had almost finished programming.

"Watch out!" she shouted. "You nearly hit Frankie."

"Seriously?" Max said. "I think you'll find that it was Frankie who nearly hit me."

"Whatever." Kensy flew the creature back to the workbench, where she donned her magnifying goggles and picked up a tiny screwdriver. "Do you like her name? I called my bee Ferdinand. They make a cute couple, don't you think?"

"What was that noise before?" Max asked, glancing around the room, wondering how

Kensy could have blown something up when she was working on a drone.

"Doesn't matter," she replied.

Max decided he wouldn't push her. He didn't want to get into an argument and he had a secret of his own now too.

"Have you looked at Grand-mère and Grand-père's potions yet?"

Kensy shook her head. "I've been way too busy with this, but I was thinking I could work a potion into the design – not deadly, of course, but something that packs a decent punch."

There had been another parcel when they'd arrived home that afternoon, but this time it was from their grandparents. It contained half a dozen small bottles with ornate botanical labels and cryptic notes on little cards hanging from their necks. Their grandparents were clearly having some fun. The twins had discovered during the week they'd spent with Hector and Marisol at Alexandria that both of them had a wicked sense of humor. There was something about the pretty packaging of the vials that didn't quite marry with the text.

Max read the letter again.

When used wisely, these scents we have
sent will make perfect sense. Enjoy!
Love, Grand-mère and Grand-père xx

"*Laughter is the Best Medicine,*" Kensy read aloud. "I bet this one gives you the giggles." She investigated another of the cards, which was attached to an amber bottle. "*On the Nose* . . . Hmm, maybe it's a nasty smell."

"Let's avoid that one for now," said Max. He inspected the next vial along, which was light blue. "*The Truth Will Set You Free.* That's easy — it must be a truth serum."

Kensy rubbed her hands together, her eyes gleaming. "We could spray some on Song and he could tell us all of Pharos's secrets."

"I can only imagine how happy Granny would be about that," Max said.

"You're no fun." Kensy picked up a light-pink vial. "This one's called *Loved-up.* Seems self-explanatory. I could spray some on you and then you'd fall head over heels for Autumn, the way she's in love with you and she'd be my best friend forever."

"She's not in love with me!" Max retorted. "We're just friends, and she's probably going to be your best friend forever anyway."

"True," Kensy teased, jumping out of his reach. She considered the final two bottles, one red and one purple. They were labeled *Sleeping Beauty* and *Get Set for a Sting in the Tail*. "I'd say this one could be perfect for Ferdinand's sting and the other one sends the target to sleep."

"Do you want to try one?" Max asked.

Kensy shrugged. "Why not? Let's put a tiny bit into Frankie then I can give her a run too. We can attack Song. He's a good sport. How about the truth serum? I promise I'll only ask boring questions like why he loves country music so much and who he thinks is the best-looking twin out of him and Sidney."

Max unscrewed the pump spray from the top of the bottle while Kensy inserted a miniature funnel into Frankie's abdomen. She had worked out how to emit a mist from the end, so long as everything operated as she had planned. Carefully, the pair worked together to fill the tiny crevice. Max replaced the lid and Kensy grabbed the controller and her glasses, which she used to maneuver the creature.

"Here goes," she said as the two exited the room. Kensy popped Frankie, the remote control and her glasses into the pockets of her lab coat.

Just as they were heading for the stairs, they heard the elevator doors open and Granny Cordelia's voice.

"Fitz should be back by now. Let's go to the dining room. We can speak in private," the woman said. There was an edge to her voice that caused them to take pause.

"I have a bad feeling about Harry and Jamila. Neither of them is unreliable," said a man they didn't recognize.

"One missing journalist and you could probably assume he was on a secret assignment somewhere, but two . . . I can't help but fear the worst." That voice belonged to their father.

"And we're still no closer to finding out

who the shooter was on the river the other night. Perhaps this is payback for the fact that they missed you," Cordelia said. "Though neither Harry nor Jamila are agents."

Kensy looked at her brother and grinned. "I think we've found the perfect testing ground for Frankie."

"What? No!" Max hissed, grabbing her by the arm. "It sounds like they're talking about something really important and confidential."

"My point exactly." Kensy wrestled her arm out of his grasp. "You have to decide – are you a spy or a scaredy-cat?"

"Fine, just don't blame me when Granny goes nuts about us eavesdropping," Max said as the pair hurried up the stairs.

The children were surprised to see the group gathered in the kitchen. As Ed looked over, it was hard to miss the concern etched into his features. "Hi, kids, what have you been up to?"

Max grinned. "Just studying."

Fitz emerged from the pantry, munching on a cookie, which he sheepishly finished when he realized they had company.

"Hello, darlings," Cordelia said. "Come and meet Peter."

Max offered his hand to the man and introduced himself. Kensy did the same.

"You might remember he was at Alexandria at Christmas, but I suspect it was all a little overwhelming. He's the editor-in-chief of the *Beacon* and has been my right-hand man for many years now."

Peter was quite a deal shorter than their father, and older too. He had thinning gray hair combed over from left to right and wore a brown suede jacket, navy trousers and black lace-up brogues. He had the look of someone with no time to waste, a man whose life ran on deadlines. Even standing there in the kitchen, his fingers were twitching, as if he had to get something done right away.

"How are you settling back into life in London?" he asked.

"Good," Max said, and Kensy nodded. "We've got our first Pharos review coming up."

Peter grimaced. "Oh, I remember those days. I always dreaded the physical activity component and I think it's much harder now — at least we never had to leap across tall buildings. Good luck."

Max gulped, wondering just how difficult it was going to be, but the idea brought a wry smile to Kensy's face.

Ed excused the group and ushered them upstairs to the ground floor of the house, where they headed for the dining room.

Song promised he would follow soon with their tea and coffee.

"Where are you two going?" he asked as the children charged upstairs too.

"To study, of course," Kensy called.

The children waited until the adults had disappeared down the hall before they scurried after them.

But the door to the dining room was firmly shut. "Any ideas?" Max looked at his sister. They didn't have to wait long.

Song walked around the corner, carrying a tea tray. The twins ducked down behind a ceramic urn and watched as he opened the door. Kensy put on her glasses, adjusted her earpiece, then pulled the controller and Frankie from her pocket.

"Here we go," she said, pressing the button to bring the creature to life.

"Just make sure that no one sees you – or we'll both be toast," Max whispered.

His sister flew the creature through the open door, narrowly avoiding a collision with the top of Song's head before she landed it on the sideboard, next to a pot.

"Are you still going to release the mist?" Max whispered as Song returned to the hallway and disappeared out of sight.

Kensy nodded and pressed the button, hoping that the diffuser worked. "Might as well. Although I think they'll probably all tell the truth anyway, so it might not have any noticeable effect."

She could hear everyone inside the room speaking loud and clear and she could see her grandmother holding court at the end of the table through Frankie's eyes, which contained a tiny camera.

"What are they saying?" Max asked.

Kensy shushed her brother with her finger. "Two journalists have gone missing from the *Beacon*," she whispered. "Harry Stokes and Jamila Assad. Apparently, Jamila received a call from Harry a few days ago, asking her to look after his cat while he pursued a big story. He'd claimed to be calling from a train, but she could hear playground noises in the background. Peter says that Harry is nuts about his cat and treats it like a child. He thinks it's strange that he would just go away and leave the animal."

Suddenly, the door opened and Fitz peered out into the hallway. The twins froze. He looked left and right, then stepped back inside and closed the door.

"Let's go to my room," Max said. "You can come and get Frankie afterward. You'll still be able to hear and see what's going on, but at least we have less chance of getting caught."

Not a minute later, Kensy plonked down on Max's bed, pushing the coding books out of the way while Max began to tidy up. He had already hidden the page he'd taken from

Magoo's office inside one of his notebooks. He wasn't sure why he didn't want to share it yet. Maybe it was pride, but he also wanted to decipher it before he told his sister. She'd only worry anyway and become more paranoid than usual with her wild theories.

Kensy was listening intently and closed her left eye so she could get a better view through the small lens on her glasses. She giggled. "I think the truth serum works. Dad just told Granny to stop being so bossy, Granny almost fell off her chair and Fitz announced that he needs to break wind." Kensy howled with laughter, clutching her sides. "He just did and it was really loud! Now he's apologizing and said he didn't know what made him say and do that."

Max chuckled. "Imagine if that was Granny."

"Shush, shush." Kensy held up her hand, still giggling. "Jamila Assad has been gone for a couple of days, but she called to tell Peter she was sick. He said he could hear playground noises in the background too, which was odd because, when he checked where she lived, it was nowhere near a school or a park. Granny has assigned Fitz to the case. There's been no ransom demands."

"Have they said anything about what stories the pair has been working on?" Max said, as he re-shelved his books and picked up the ones from the floor.

Kensy shook her head. "They're leaving." She watched through her glasses and saw her grandmother and Peter go first then her father. Kensy was about to activate Frankie when she saw Fitz staring straight at her.

"Where did you come from?" he said, and reached for the butterfly.

Kensy lifted the creature into the air and it fluttered out the door and upstairs. She met Frankie in the hallway and quickly stuffed her in her underwear drawer along with the glasses and remote control. No one would ever find them among that mess.

CHAPTER 9

.— .—. ——— ——— ..—. — ——— .—.
—.—. . ...— — .. . .——

The rest of the week flew by. When the twins weren't at school, they were at home studying for their review, poring over textbooks and notes, or in the basement, training with Song or tinkering with projects in the workshop and laboratory. Mr. Nutting had made good on his offer to help them with some extra training after school, and Mrs. Vanden Boom had been incredibly generous coaching the twins on their chemistry, in particular. Monty Reffell had given them a couple of hours on plots and strategies too, although the logic behind him delivering the lesson dressed as Napoleon had been lost on Kensy and Max.

In the little bit of spare time Max had, he'd been working on the coded message from Magoo's office, but progress was slow. Their mother had been just as busy, studying for her exams, and they'd barely seen their father or Fitz. No one had told them about the missing journalists and, given they'd found out via surreptitious means, they didn't imagine it was a good idea to ask.

"Okay," Song said. "I think it is time for some parkour training." The man was wearing a navy apron and pink rubber gloves and was standing at the sink, where he was up to his elbows in dirty dishes.

Max looked over from the kitchen table, where he was writing chemistry notes on synthesis and direct combustion. Kensy was sitting opposite him, looking for codes in this evening's edition of the *Beacon*.

"You mean downstairs on the VR device?" the boy asked.

The children had eaten with Song since their mother had gone to the university to meet with one of her old professors, their father and grandmother were in Edinburgh on business and who knew where Fitz was.

Song removed his rubber gloves and placed some plastic wrap over the lasagna dish. "No, you have been doing very well in the virtual world, but tonight I believe we should try some live action," he replied.

"Where?" Kensy asked.

"I have a place," Song said with a glint in his eye.

Max's stomach flipped. "That sounds dangerous."

"It sounds exciting." Kensy tossed aside the newspaper. She had been working from the real estate section without any luck.

Song nodded. "Confucius says success depends upon previous preparation, and without such preparation there is sure to be failure. It is about time we test this theory out in the world. Upstairs in your wardrobes you will find pants, hoodies and shoes – all black.

Get changed and meet me here in ten minutes, and think about whether you have any small equipment that might be useful."

The twins pushed out their chairs and raced each other up the stairs, hurtling back to the kitchen in record time. Song had changed too.

"Are you a ninja, Song?" Kensy giggled as the man walked out of the butler's pantry clad from head to toe in black with a small backpack over his shoulder and a black beanie on his head.

The man grinned. "Let's go."

Minutes later, the three were in a cab, navigating the streets of London while Song explained exactly what they were about to do.

Kensy looked across at him. "So, you're serious about this?"

"Deadly," the man replied.

The traffic had thinned from the evening peak, although there were still plenty of commuters and tourists on the streets. Max couldn't help thinking it was far too early to be attempting an activity requiring stealth.

"How long have we got?" he asked.

"As this is your first time out in the field, I will give you thirty minutes to make your way from Fortnum & Mason to Lillywhites –"

"Um, we walked there the other day and it took five minutes," Max said. "Half the time if we ran."

Song smiled. "Without touching the ground."

The cheeky grin evaporated from the lad's face.

"So it's rooftops only?" Kensy said. "We can do that. The buildings all butt up against one another, don't they?"

Max thought for a moment, his eyes widening. "Regent Street separates the end of the block from Lillywhites. We can't possibly jump that far . . . and there's St. James's Church too, which has a lot of land around it."

"Mmm," Song said. "Then you must find another way."

The taxi pulled up in Duke Street, down the side of Fortnum & Mason near another rear alley.

Kensy glanced around at the people milling

about. "And you couldn't have thought of a place where we might attract less attention?"

"Of course," Song replied, "but this is much more fun. Your adrenaline will be pumping, I can assure you. I was there for your father and Fitz's first rooftop run as well. They had to negotiate their way to the bell tower at St. Paul's from the outside of the building." Song chuckled at the memory, as did the driver.

Kensy and Max recognized the man from Alexandria, but they weren't allowed to utter his name – even if they did remember it.

"Okay," Kensy said, steeling herself, "if Dad and Fitz could do that then we can get from one end of Piccadilly to the other without getting caught or killed."

Song pulled out two headsets and what looked like night-vision goggles from his backpack. "You will wear these. I will be able to see exactly what you are seeing too. And if you get into any trouble, your safe word is 'home' and I will send a retrieval team."

"A retrieval team?" Kensy's eyebrows

jumped up. "Like a helicopter or something?"

Song shook his head. "Me – I will come and get you. So do not get yourselves into trouble – my climbing skills are not what they used to be."

"Is someone going to let us into the building so we can get to the roof?" Max asked.

Song shook his head again and pointed.

"We're climbing?" The boy caught the gist of what the man was getting at.

"We will be waiting for you at the other end." Song grinned. "Good luck. Your time starts . . . now."

* * *

Kensy shimmied up the drainpipe ahead of her brother, hoping that the building maintenance was as good as it looked. The last thing she wanted was for the pipe to come away from the wall. It took no time at all to get to the roof of Fortnum & Mason and it was pretty straightforward from there, as they raced to the Piccadilly side. They had to keep low as the buildings opposite were a similar height, but at least there was no moon overhead tonight.

They reached the edge and realized the next roof was pitched. It belonged to Hatchard's, the oldest bookshop in the city. Max jumped down first, and the twins balanced with the sure-footedness of tightrope walkers along the ridge capping. Once they reached the next roof, it was plain sailing. They ran and leapt without impediment, but that was all about to come to an end when they reached the Maison Assouline building.

"Stay close," Max called to his sister as they approached the edge.

Kensy suddenly realized the rooftops had run out. "Where now?"

Max pointed down at the wall below. "There."

"That's fine for the first part," Kensy said. "What about past the gate? The iron spikes."

"Just don't slip," Max said.

Kensy frowned. "There are people everywhere. They're going to see us."

"We're kids — maybe they won't notice,

and it is pretty dark," Max said, crossing his fingers as the pair leapt to a ledge below. Next, they dropped a few feet to a generous windowsill and then swung onto the top of the wall.

Kensy flew along with Max behind her, like two circus performers hoping no one had caught sight of their act.

A little boy wearing a navy puffer jacket and beanie pointed up at them. "Dad, look – ninjas!" But by the time the man pulled his phone away from his ear, Kensy and Max were well past the pair, clambering over the iron gate and making long leaps between the posts to the flat pillars that supported them.

"The drainpipe," Kensy called to Max.

He nodded and made his way past a window and shimmied up. This time it was trickier to get a grip as the pipe was rectangular, not round.

The children were on a roof again in no time, but there was an alley separating the next two buildings. They were going to have to jump across then scale the outside to the top. It was fortunate that the shops and apartments of London had been built during a time when ornate plasterwork demanded ledges and deep windowsills with overhangs, so at least there was something to grip on to.

Max made the run-up first. He took off into the air, his arms spinning like the blades of a windmill, and landed with a crunch on a window ledge. Realizing there was someone inside, he pressed himself against the wall, out of sight.

Kensy leapt down to join him. She almost lost her balance, teetering for a second before steadying herself. Unfortunately, she was on the other side of the window and had to cross it to get to where they were going next.

"There's someone in there," Max hissed.

Just as Kensy was about to step across, the window opened and they heard a woman's voice complaining that there was no air in the apartment. Kensy peered around. The woman had walked away into the next room, but there was a little girl sitting on a mat on the floor. She couldn't have been more than two or three, and when she spotted Kensy she squealed. Kensy did a little dance, trying to distract the kid, but she was a screamer.

The woman ran back into the room at the exact moment Kensy leapt across the window then followed Max up to the next ledge and onto the roof. The boy's arms and legs were aching, and his heart was pumping so hard he thought it was going to burst through his chest, but they couldn't stop now.

He checked his watch. "We've got ten minutes left."

"I hope that lady doesn't call the police," Kensy panted.

Back on the rooftops, it was much easier going. They flew across the metal, jumping down from one level to the next. As they ran across the front of the Waterstones building, Kensy looked sideways and realized there was a book launch happening in the room that opened onto the roof. She could see a huge poster – the novel was called *Spy Games*. Several people glanced her way, so she did the only reasonable thing – a cartwheel – then pressed a finger to her lips, hoping they would think it was all part of the event.

"Alley alert!" Max shouted to his sister as they raced on. This time the adjacent roof was lower and there was grass around the edges. He landed on his feet. Kensy followed but was a little off balance and commando rolled as she hit the ground.

Max turned. "You okay?" he called.

Kensy nodded and dusted herself off.

"We've got five minutes," the boy urged.

The pair reached the edge of the last building, but this time the gap wasn't an alley — it was two wide sidewalks on either side of a three-lane road. There was no way they could jump that distance.

"We're not allowed to climb down and run across the street," Max said, trying to think of options. "And leaping this far onto the roof of a bus or truck is a death wish."

"I have this." Kensy pulled a tiny device from her pocket. It looked like a miniature tape measure. She'd grabbed it from the workshop on the way out — one of the many inventions

Granny Cordelia had left for them to use or improve.

Back in the taxi, Song smiled. He had been joined by Gordon Nutting, who was also watching the children's progress.

"Well done, Miss Kensington," Song said.

Gordon grinned. "Very impressive."

There was a metal railing running around the top of the building. Kensy pulled and pushed to make sure it was secure, then fastened the device to it and lined up her target – a high section of wall jutting out from the roof opposite. The side of the building was covered in plastic and scaffolding, so at least it wasn't currently worthy of tourist photos.

"Will it reach that far?" Max asked, biting his lip.

"I hope so," Kensy said, and took aim. The cable launched into the air across the street and thudded into the target. Kensy gave a pull to make sure it was taut. She reached into her hoodie pocket for a leather strap and gave another to Max. Then she placed her hands through the loops and wrapped them securely. "Wish me luck, little brother," she said, and ran toward the edge of the building, zip-lining across the open street below and landing on the Lillywhites roof.

Max glanced at his watch. He had less than a minute.

"Hey, what do you think you're doing?" a gravelly voice shouted.

Max turned and saw a burly security guard running toward him. There was no time. He had to go now. He took off, whizzing across Regent Street toward his sister, and landed with a thud. Kensy pressed the release button, which sent the silica nanofiber cable hurtling toward them, winding as it went so that, by the time Kensy put out her hand to catch it, the device was fully retracted.

"I'm calling the police!" the man yelled from the other rooftop. But Kensy and Max had already made their way down the scaffolding inside its white plastic cover. As they reached the ground, a taxi pulled up right next to them. Song opened the door and leaned out.

The children jumped inside and the vehicle took off into the evening traffic.

"How did we do?" Max looked at the man and realized he wasn't alone. "Hello, Mr. Nutting – what are you doing here?"

Kensy pulled off her beanie and wiped her brow. Despite the chilly evening air, her hair was plastered to the sides of her face.

The PE teacher and weapons specialist grinned. "Well done, children. Congratulations on passing the parkour section of your review."

"That was part of our review?!" Kensy glared at the butler. "You could have told us before."

"You would have only been more stressed. I think it was for the best, although I had to intercept a call from a woman who tried to report your presence to the police," Song said.

Kensy grimaced. "Sorry about that."

"All in a day's work," Song replied. "Mr. Nutting, would you like to join us at home for some celebratory ice cream?"

"Song's been testing some really cool flavors,"

Max jumped in. "Chocolate honeycomb's my current favorite."

"His passion fruit and mint is amazing too," Kensy said.

"That sounds wonderful," Gordon Nutting replied. "It's not often I get to eat ice cream in peace with five little ones about."

"That's settled then. Home, please," Song said to the driver.

CHAPTER 10

— ——— —— —— — ——— ——— ——— —— —
——— —— ——— — — —— ——— —

Elliot Frizzle's smile was as bright as his magenta jacket. Paired with a lime-green shirt, navy tie and pants, he certainly wasn't going to be missed.

"You look happy, sir. Is it the weather?" Carlos commented as the children filed into the art room, its white walls covered in various student masterpieces. The benches around the perimeter were filled with all manner of works-in-progress, from pottery to wire sculptures and puppets, and the sinks at the back of the room were splattered with paint.

"Certainly a little bit of spring sunshine does tend to improve one's disposition," the man replied.

But that wasn't the only reason he was feeling upbeat. He'd just been given the go-ahead for the *Romeo and Juliet* set design he'd been working away at for the past couple of weeks. Theo Richardson said he loved the concept and Magoo was equally enamored. Elliot couldn't wait to get to work, but that would have to happen after hours, of course. Thankfully, he'd already told Eric Lazenby, the school custodian and resident handyman, to make a start on construction days ago and the man had created most of the backdrop in his workshop at school. It could have been awkward if Theo had rejected the design, but Elliot was brimming with confidence. He'd shared the images with Lottie Ziegler, who thought a professional theater production would be lucky to have anything as good. Elliott would do the painting here at school and the set would be transported to the theater once it was done.

"We're going to be doing some still-life

drawing today," Elliot said, and disappeared into the storeroom.

A tiny blonde girl called Evelyn looked up in horror. "Doesn't that mean drawing naked people? I'm not doing that. Nudity is gross, especially if they're as old as my granny, who likes to take off her clothes in the back garden all the time. Dad says she looks like she needs ironing."

There was a chortle of nervous laughter around the class and some hearty agreement.

Kensy rolled her eyes and perched on a stool. "Well, unless Moretti's volunteering, I think we're probably drawing a basket of fruit or something. Let's face it, none of us want to see him in the buff."

Carlos chuckled. "Good one, Kensy."

Mr. Frizzle emerged from the storeroom with a bowl containing half a dozen green apples, much to the relief of the class. He demonstrated some artistic techniques on an easel at the front of the room, then told the children to have a go, and he'd come around and give them some tips.

Autumn leaned across to Kensy. "Mr.

Richardson said the cast list for the play would be up on the bulletin board this afternoon – I can't wait to see if I got in," she whispered. They had to speak in hushed tones as Mr. Frizzle dictated they work silently while listening to music. Today he was playing Puccini, which was already hurting Kensy's head. "I heard him in the hallway earlier talking about it to Mr. Reffell and Madame Verte – he was like a six-year-old at Christmas. They didn't seem nearly as keen, and I heard Mr. Reffell asking him why it all had to happen so quickly. Apparently, the play will be on in a few weeks, which means there will be loads of time out of class for rehearsals, but it has something to do with being able to use the Victoria Theatre."

Kensy drew another circle and began to shade the side. "I don't care about the silly play. My audition was so awful I'd be lucky to get a gig on the stage crew. But at least Mr. Richardson was kind about my efforts and didn't make me feel like a complete fool. Maybe he's not as bad as I first thought."

Autumn grinned at her friend. "I told you

he's lovely."

Kensy leaned back and considered her apples, which she decided looked more like bottoms. "One kind word does not maketh a superhuman being – he still loves himself to death," she said, and took to the paper with an eraser.

* * *

The students clamored around the bulletin board with whoops of joy and sighs of disappointment. There weren't too many surprises, although Kensy did enjoy seeing the look on Blair's face when the role of Juliet went to Misha. Blair was The Nurse. Max had earned himself the part of The Chorus, an all-knowing narrator, which he was glad to learn took place entirely off stage. Autumn won the part of Lady Capulet while Dante was Mercutio and Carlos was playing Paris. Harper was Lady Montague and Yasmina was Rosaline. The role of Romeo had surprisingly gone to Alfie. The cast was a mix of trainee agents and regular students, which is exactly how Mr. MacGregor would have wanted it.

"I told you I wouldn't get in," Kensy said, regretting that she had delivered such a poor audition.

Autumn looked at her friend. "I'm sorry you didn't get a part. It won't be the same without you."

"I'm relieved," Kensy fibbed, mustering a smile. "At least I'll have time to study. I'm definitely going to beat Max in our reviews."

But, truth be told, Kensy was disappointed, especially as the other kids were all congratulating each other and talking about how much fun it was going to be.

Theo Richardson was hovering in the background and called out that the cast and stage crew were to meet him on Monday afternoon for the first rehearsal. Autumn set off to see Madame Verte about some extra revision for her upcoming Mandarin exam.

"Hey, Kens," Max called, but his sister chose to ignore him.

"Someone's peeved," Carlos said.

"She didn't want to be in it in the first

place," Max replied. "She only auditioned because Fitz said it would be good to test her acting skills."

Kensy opened her locker and dragged out her backpack. Unfortunately, as she did, the rest of the contents spilled onto the floor. "Seriously?" she fumed, and kicked at a folder before turning around to see Mr. Richardson bent on the ground, gathering her belongings. Kensy felt her cheeks light up. "Sorry, sir," she mumbled sheepishly as he passed her a pile of books.

"Would you still like some extra help with what we were practicing the other day?" the teacher asked.

Kensy nodded. "That would be great, but I don't think you're going to have time now that the play is underway."

"I've got an idea," Theo said with a grin. "Come and see me on Monday before school and we can chat. I think you're going to enjoy this."

Kensy stuffed her things into the locker and leaned against the door, snapping it shut. She wondered exactly what he had in mind.

CHAPTER 11

—•—•• •• ——•—•• •••• — ••• ——••••— —

—•—•• •— —— •••• •— ••• ——••••—

—•—• ——— —— •—•—• ——— ••• ••• •—•— •

"Max, how do you feel about living in London, after having spent your entire life on the move around the globe?" Fitz asked, looking at the boy intently.

Max leaned forward in his seat. "It's been a transition, but it's nice to be in the one place for a while and put down roots. It definitely helps with making friends at school too."

"Brilliant, mate. You'll be terrific." Fitz grinned. "Your body language conveys confidence and you're answering truthfully."

Kensy was sitting beside her brother on the couch, picking at her nails.

"Oh, Kens, what did I tell you about fidgeting?" Fitz said. "You need to sit still and look as if you're interested, even if you'd rather be at home giving Song a pedicure."

She flinched at the very thought of it. "I don't want to be on television. The whole thing makes me feel sick. It's a silly idea and I don't see why Granny has to make this big announcement." The girl pouted. "Besides, everyone knows I'm a terrible actress – I didn't even get a part in the school play."

Max had tried to talk to her about it on Friday afternoon and again this morning, but Kensy had ignored him and spent the day in the laboratory, working on another insect – a dragonfly this time. Max had been busy studying upstairs and working on Magoo's code whenever he could snatch an hour. So far he thought he had one word – *future* – whatever that was supposed to mean. Whose future did it refer to? His and Kensy's? The organization's? It was driving him nuts.

Song was sitting in a chair opposite the children, pretending to be a television viewer. He shook his head. "Miss Kensington, you are coming across as a spoiled brat. We need you to be more likeable or people may not believe your parents' story."

Kensy stood up. "I hate this!" she said, and stormed into the kitchen, yanking open a freezer drawer and pulling out a tub of chocolate-chip ice cream. She grabbed a spoon and sat down at the island, digging into the container and stuffing a rather too-large amount into her mouth.

It was early Saturday afternoon and Ed had been at the paper since half past nine, catching up on work, while Anna was busy studying for her upcoming exams. Fitz had been out all morning too and had arrived home just after lunch with a thick file that he'd taken straight upstairs. He'd reappeared a little while ago to do another run-through of the questions with the children.

Max wanted to ask him about the missing journalists, but every time he thought he might, he changed his mind. The interview with Evan Pinkstone was due to take place in two hours and, while Max was a model student, Kensy's propensity for blatant honesty without a drop of truth serum was doing her no favors at all.

"Please come back and we'll go over things one more time," Fitz said.

"I will make your favorite dinner tonight, Miss Kensington – if you do as Mr. Fitz has requested," Song said with a lilt in his voice.

Kensy turned around, her frown lines deep. "With crackling and applesauce?"

"All the trimmings and not a brussels sprout in sight," Song replied with a nod.

"I thought your favorite dinner was dumplings?" Max said. He had been looking forward to them if she agreed.

"It's a girl's prerogative to change her mind," Kensy quipped, and returned the half-empty tub of ice cream to the freezer drawer. "Fine, I'll try again."

Ed walked up the stairs from the basement just as they were about to start and Anna appeared in the kitchen soon after.

"Good timing." Fitz beckoned for them to join the children. "Your mother's just sent the final questions for the interview."

Anna walked into the family room.

Kensy jumped up and hugged her. "I'm hopeless, Mum. It would be better if I didn't say anything – just pretend I'm the mute child."

Ed chuckled and sat down beside Max. "I don't think that's feasible. And, sweetheart, you are not and never have been hopeless at anything in your entire life. I suggest you keep your wits about you and just be yourself. None of this is going to be difficult. If Evan decides he wants to be a hero and ask some hard-hitting questions, your mother and I will take care of it. Whatever you do, don't panic."

"What about Fitz? Aren't you going to be part of the interview too?" Max said, realizing that all the while they'd been practicing Fitz had been the one asking questions.

Fitz shook his head. "I'll be there and your parents will talk about me, but I'm not appearing on camera — it's best this way."

"After all, Fitz has a head for radio," Ed teased.

The children snickered and Fitz feigned offense. "How can you say that with this superbly shiny noggin of mine?" he said. "Let's face it, I'm a lot more handsome than when we were in Sydney."

"Mmm." Song nodded. "But you must admit that was some of my finest work."

The mood in the room had lifted considerably in the past couple of minutes.

"So, sweetheart," Ed said, turning to his daughter, "are you ready?"

Kensy took a deep breath. "I'll do my best."

* * *

"That wasn't so bad, was it?" Anna smiled at Kensy and Max. The children were sitting between their parents on a long navy couch opposite the host of the show. Evan Pinkstone stood up and shook Edward's hand then Anna's and the children's. Fitz was nearby, having been keeping a close eye on the proceedings.

Evan grimaced. "Well, I suspect you lot are going to cause a fuss for a day or so – until another big news story comes along."

"I don't want any fuss at all," Kensy said. "It's going to be bad enough at school when *everyone* finds out. I hope Granny's strategy with the paparazzi works and we don't have anyone tailing us on motor scooters. Anyway, if they do, I've got a crash strategy."

Anna looked at her daughter in horror. "Kensy, you do not!"

"Yes, I do," the girl quipped and put her hand in her pocket. She had sneaked a few exploding tacks from school and was prepared to use them. Apparently, they were almost fail-safe when it came to blowing tires.

During the interview, the crew had been kept to a bare minimum with only a couple of cameramen, a boom operator, the director and Evan. They'd all signed confidentiality clauses as part of Cordelia's plan to maintain as much control over the delivery of the news as possible.

"Thanks for doing this, Evan," Ed said, as Anna guided the children off the set toward the studio exit. Fitz emerged too and walked toward them.

"I can't tell you what a shock I got when your mother called and offered me the exclusive." Evan shook his head. "She said that it would be worth my while, but, by gosh, I never imagined it would be her family back from the dead."

"I would have thought that in your line of work there wouldn't be many things that surprised you," Ed said.

Evan smiled. "True. Anyway, it was a pleasure, and I do appreciate your mother trusting me."

With that, the family headed back downstairs to the parking garage. Song was dutifully standing beside the taxi, waiting to escort them home.

"Well, that went okay, I think," Max said, staring out into the streets of London. It was dreary again and flecks of drizzle were hitting the windshield.

"Absolutely." Fitz looked across from the pull-down seat. "And, Kensy, you were great."

No one was going to mention that she'd almost spilled the beans about the attack at the river. Max intercepted her just in time to say that they were enjoying some lovely evening walks together as a family, getting to know the city.

"How are you doing with your study for the review?" Ed asked. "Feeling confident?"

"Getting there," Max said.

Kensy agreed.

"And I gather you've both nominated a special area of expertise now," their father said.

"Geography," Max replied. "Although it was a toss-up between that and ciphers. I think I have a bit more to learn there." Max fingered the piece of paper that he'd been carrying around everywhere. He was desperate to make more progress, but there just hadn't been time.

"Mechanical engineering for me," Kensy said, which came as no surprise to anyone.

While the review would cover general spy skills, the children had been given the opportunity to elect an area they felt proficient in. This would make up twenty percent of the assessment. Given they'd already passed the physical challenge on the rooftops, at least that was one component out of the way.

"So, Max, what's the capital of Ethiopia then?" Anna asked. She was sitting between the twins in the back seat with Ed in the pull-down seat opposite. Song was riding up front beside the driver.

Kensy looked at her mother, deadpan. "You're going to have to be trickier than that, Mum. Even I know its Addis Ababa."

"Okay, the second-largest city in New Zealand, population and latitude?" Ed said.

"Easy, that's Wellington with 418,500 people and a latitude of 41° 17' south, making it the southernmost capital city in the world," Max said. "That's a bit basic, Dad."

"Well done, Master Maxim," Song said from the front. He was listening through the intercom. "How about the twelfth largest city in Mexico by population and, for a bonus point, can you spell it?"

"Chihuahua – 809,232 at last count," the boy said.

"And it's spelled C-h-i-h-u-a-h-u-a," Kensy added.

"Excellent!" Ed reached across and patted Anna's knee. "Whoever these kids' parents are, they must be super clever to produce these two little geniuses."

Kensy and Max grinned. It was so good to be back together as a family, even if they still had a thousand unanswered questions about their parents' lives.

"So, Dad, how much of what you told Evan was true?" Max asked.

"Not a lot," the man replied.

"You know how the other night you mentioned all those people who could be after you?" Kensy said. "Can you tell us about them?"

The taxi continued to weave through the backstreets of London, past red buses and families taking cover under umbrellas after a Saturday outing.

"Who was that guy called Kodiak?" Max asked.

Song grinned to himself. "Do not forget

Delfroy. Together, they were the worst of the worst – up to terrible no good."

The twins looked at their father expectantly.

"Delfroy and Kodiak were part of a plot to blow up the palace," the man said, nodding toward the Buckingham Palace gates, which they were driving past right at that moment.

"But your father and mother and Fitz stopped them," Song said. "In fact, your mother was the one who deactivated the bomb that had been planted in Her Majesty's handbag."

"What?" Kensy was incredulous. "No way."

"Anna swapped her bag with the Queen's, then took it to the powder room," Ed said proudly. "Thankfully, your mother knew exactly what to do."

Anna shook her head. "I thought we were all going to die that night – let's just say I got lucky with the red and green wires. Your father and Fitz apprehended Delfroy and Kodiak and handed them over to MI5."

"Why were you at the palace in the first place?" Max asked.

"We'd been invited to a ball, but we were

there for a little bit more than dancing," Fitz said. "We'd been trailing these guys for over a year and suspected they were going to act that night."

Kensy gazed at her mother with new eyes. "You're incredible."

Anna's face tightened. "No, I'm not. I just did what was required and, believe me, I much prefer living the quiet life. Pharos is not all glamour and parties – there have been far too many times I didn't know if your father would be coming home to me."

Ed looked at his wife, a peculiar expression on his face.

"Please tell us more," Max said. "I want to hear *all* the stories."

"Later," Ed said, noting his wife's frown.

The car pulled up outside the basement apartment in John Islip Street and, one by one, the family hopped out. Kensy was just about to head down the stairs when she realized that the front door was ajar. She stopped suddenly and was almost toppled over by her brother.

"What did you do that for?" he barked,

but Kensy turned and shushed him with her finger. The trouble was, Song and Fitz were still chattering away.

"Stop talking, everyone!" she hissed, and pointed downstairs.

Fitz understood at once. He looked to Ed, who turned his palms upward. "I've got nothing."

Anna's heart was pounding. She was glad to hear that her husband hadn't taken a gun to the television station. It would have caused havoc with security.

"Do you think it could have something to do with the speedboat?" Max whispered to his sister.

Song pulled a small pistol from a holster inside his jacket and handed it to Fitz, who tiptoed down the stairs with Ed close behind him. The man hesitated for a moment before he pushed open the door. He could see the silhouette of a man leaning over the hall table.

"I suggest you don't move," Fitz said, pointing the gun.

Startled, the man dropped the file he was

holding on the floor.

"It's me, Peter!" He spun around, much to the relief of Fitz and Ed.

"Good grief, man." Fitz lowered the gun. "What were you thinking, leaving the door open?"

"Did I?" Peter turned and realized that the whole family was now standing in the dimly lit hallway.

Song flicked on the light and closed the front door.

"You've seen better days," Ed said to their guest. Long strands of hair had escaped from Peter's comb-over and were hanging untidily from the left side of his face and he had puffy bags under his eyes.

"I haven't been sleeping much," he said. "I just came to drop off some more stories from the archives – I've been raking through everything, but I must be too close to it. I can't make heads or tails of anything anymore."

Kensy nudged her brother. "Is something the matter?" she asked innocently.

"It's none of your concern, Kens," Ed said.

Fitz eyeballed the girl. "But you know already, don't you?" Kensy shook her head and tried to act innocent, but Fitz knew better. "I saw your drone in the dining room the other day."

Kensy smiled sheepishly. "Okay, you got me, but I didn't act alone and we've kept it secret. Anyway, maybe we can help?"

"We could take a look at the newspaper articles," Max added. "Be two sets of fresh eyes."

"You have a review to study for," Anna protested.

But the twins argued what better way to learn than to work on an actual case.

"I suggest we head to the house and I will make some tea," Song said. "I also have a dinner to finish preparing."

Peter turned to leave. "I'll get going."

Ed placed a hand on the weary man's shoulder. "Have dinner with us tonight, and I think you should stay in the guest room. Get some rest, or you'll be no use to anyone."

Peter sighed but didn't argue. Sometimes

it was good to be told what to do rather than always be the one in charge. "That sounds grand. Thank you."

Minutes later, they were back at number thirteen with the kettle on and pages scattered all over the kitchen table.

CHAPTER 12

—·—· ——— —·—·—·· —·—· —·—

Kensy and Max spent Sunday morning sifting through the newspaper archives, trying to piece together any connections between the stories Harry Stokes and Jamila Assad had filed in recent years. Their father, Peter and Fitz had joined them for a little while then left the house to follow some potential leads. Apparently, there had been no communication from the pair at all and it was getting harder to explain their absence in the newsroom. Jamila's mother had called the office to ask if Peter could pass on a message to make sure that her daughter remembered her cousin's bridal shower next weekend – fortunately, it wasn't unusual for the woman to be busy with work and not return her mother's calls. If they weren't found soon, though, they would have to involve the police and that was a story the *Beacon* certainly didn't want to break.

By lunchtime, the twins had given up looking for clues, deciding to use the afternoon to study separately in their rooms. Max was also learning his lines for the play ahead of their first rehearsal tomorrow. Anna had been locked away all day too, knee-deep in the latest technological advances in hip replacements, fractures and breaks, given that her specialization was orthopedics and her first examination was bone setting.

Kensy's stomach grumbled and she slammed her textbook shut. She wandered down the hall to her brother's room, where, despite his studying, there was barely a thing out of place – unlike her own room, which looked like it had been hit by a tornado.

Max was sitting at his desk and didn't hear her come in. "Where did you come from?" he gasped, when she poked her head over his shoulder.

"My stealth skills must be improving." The girl grinned and snatched up Magoo's coded message. "What's this?"

"Nothing important," Max lied.

Kensy scanned the page. "Looks like chicken scratchings to me," she said, and threw it back down. Max breathed a sigh of relief and quickly folded the page, stuffing it into his jeans pocket. He'd taken photographic evidence but was planning to make some copies too, just in case it got lost.

"Song said that Granny is coming over to watch the show with us," Max said, hoping to divert his sister's attention.

"Really?" Kensy frowned. "I still hate the idea of it. What if the paparazzi start following us tomorrow? It wouldn't be that hard to find out where we go to school and then they'd know where we live – sort of. It's bad enough that Mum and Dad and Fitz already have a list of people a mile long who want to kill them. Wasn't that story about the palace amazing?"

Max nodded. "We'll just have to cross that bridge if we come to it, Kens – and Granny had a plan, remember? I'm sure she has all bases covered." He stood up and put his books back on the shelf. "It's too late now, anyway – the show's on in half an hour. Come on. I'm starving."

The children followed the smell of curry to the kitchen, where Song was just taking papadums and naan out of the oven. The island was laid out with several dishes: beef vindaloo, tandoori lamb, homemade raita and Kensy's favorite, butter chicken.

Fitz and Ed were back from wherever they'd gone and Anna had just arrived in the kitchen.

"Please help yourselves. Tonight, I will make a special exception and permit you all to eat dinner in front of the television," Song said.

"Promise we won't make a mess," Fitz said, raising his fingers in a Scout's salute.

The family was soon perched along the sectional sofa. Song joined them too, eager to watch the interview.

"Yoo-hoo!" a cheery voice called up the basement stairs. "Golly, I'll be glad when I can use the front door – that really is taking the long way round."

"Granny!" Kensy practically hurled her plate onto the coffee table and leapt off the couch, almost kicking her father in the head as she executed the jump.

"Steady on." Ed shook his head and wiped the orange blob of butter chicken from his trousers with his finger.

"Hello, darlings," Cordelia said, breezing into the kitchen with Kensy wrapped around her. "I've brought a box of Sidney's melting moments and I have presents from Mim, Hector and Marisol. They've been very busy and want the children to test some more of their latest inventions. I believe they already posted a parcel of special scents to you, but they've added a couple more."

"Cool!" Max jumped off the couch and

ran over to inspect the little bottles Cordelia had pulled out of a bag.

"Gin and tonic, ma'am?" Song asked.

"That would be lovely, Song. And I would adore some of that butter chicken and naan – it smells delicious. Would you mind bringing me a plate? I'll go and join everyone on the couch," she said.

Song nodded. "Of course, ma'am."

Kensy studied the labels on the new vials. "*Grizzle and Groan* – that sounds weird, as if it would make someone really grumpy. Better not try that on Miss Witherbee – she's in a bad mood enough of the time already."

The other vial contained something called *The Madness Mix*, which seemed particularly ominous.

"Are you all going to come and watch this?" Fitz called as the breaking news theme blared.

"I hope that's not about us," Max said, hurrying back to the couch. Cordelia and Kensy followed him and found their spots while Song passed the woman a fork and plate and set her crystal tumbler down on the coffee table.

"In breaking news this evening, Titus Farrow, lead singer of chart-topping group Scandal, has created his own scandal by biting his girlfriend's dog on the ear while dining in Lilac Bloomfield's Michelin-starred restaurant. The man was arrested for cruelty to animals and bringing a dog into a prohibited venue. According to witnesses, the canine was concealed in Titus's girlfriend's oversized handbag. He is out on bail and will appear in court tomorrow morning. On a brighter note, tonight's weather will be fine, getting down to a low of forty degrees, and tomorrow is looking sunny with a high temperature of sixty-five. Enjoy your evening and, please, try not to snack on your pets. Good night."

"Seriously, who bites a dog on the ear? That's disgusting!" Kensy grimaced.

The theme song for Evan's show played next and the family was glued to the screen, watching the twenty-minute exposé. Evan had stuck to the script with his questions and Anna and Ed's responses made as much sense as faking your deaths in a fiery plane crash and spending the past eleven years moving their family all over the world could. The one thing that wasn't completely resolved was why they were able to come home, though it was intimated that the person responsible for the threats in the first place was no longer alive. That technically wasn't true. The reason they were back was that, when Anna and Ed disappeared to look for Hector and Marisol, Fitz had no option but to take the children home. It was part of the deal about them leaving in the first place – if anything ever happened to Anna and Ed, Fitz had to take the children to Cordelia. Things just played out from there and now they were back for good.

"Well, that wasn't so bad," Cordelia said, wiping her mouth with a napkin. "I must say I have a very good-looking family – the camera adored you all."

"That's why Fitz wasn't on screen with us – Dad says he's got a head for radio." Max chuckled and his father turned and high-fived the boy.

Fitz rolled his eyes. "Lovely, isn't it? My own flesh and blood."

"Now, I don't want anyone worrying about what might happen tomorrow – I'm afraid to be a party pooper, but I'm almost certain there will be a much bigger story than your return – maybe even two or three," Cordelia said. "Song, thank you for the curry – it was delicious, as always, but I best be going. Would you mind calling Sidney to come and collect me?"

Kensy frowned. "Do you have to go already?"

"Oh, darling, when you get as old as I am, you'll need your beauty sleep too," the woman said. "Well done, everyone – I'm very proud of you all." Cordelia stood up to leave. "Oh, there is one more thing. We're off to a book launch tomorrow evening. It's for a dear friend and I thought it a good opportunity to reintroduce my family to society."

Anna's eyes widened. "But the children have school the next day and I have an exam at the end of the week. They can't have a late night."

"We'll only be an hour or so," Cordelia said. "It's important to me. I'd much rather you and the children were there than me fielding questions on your behalf."

Anna looked to her husband for support, but Ed simply shrugged. "Mother, I'm afraid Fitz and I won't be able to make it."

Cordelia looked at her son. "I didn't expect you would."

Anna could feel her temperature rising. It was just like her mother-in-law to let Ed off the hook – as if his work was *so* much more important than hers. "I really don't think it's a good idea," Anna insisted, her fingernails digging into her palms.

"As I said, it will only be an hour and the children will have to meet my friends outside the organization at some stage. You know as well as I do how complicated life is in our position. Song, you'll bring Anna and the twins. I'll send you the location. The event starts at seven, and I guarantee you'll be home by quarter past eight. And I believe Song has a lovely outfit arranged for you, dear. Please wear it."

Anna flinched. The air could have been cut with a knife.

Cordelia farewelled the family and Song escorted her downstairs to Sidney, who was waiting in the car in John Islip Street.

Back at number thirteen, Anna sat on the sofa, staring at the television set. She was doing her best to stop the tears that were welling in her eyes.

"Are you okay, Mum?" Max asked, shuffling closer to her on the sofa.

"I wish we'd never come back!" she blurted, and jumped off the couch and fled upstairs.

"Mum!" Max called after her. He scrambled off the sofa and ran to the bottom of the stairs, but she'd already disappeared.

"Leave her, mate," Ed said gently. "I'll go up in a few minutes."

Max felt his stomach churning.

"Why do Granny and Mum hate each other?" Kensy asked, using her finger to mop up the last of the sauce on her plate.

Song was busy packaging the leftovers in the kitchen. "Confucius says behind every smile there are teeth," he said with a nod.

Kensy frowned. "Okay, you've got me. What's that supposed to mean?"

Max walked over and began rinsing dishes and packing them into the dishwasher. "Is it something about Mum and Granny being proud and they both want what's best for us, so they sometimes clash? They smile, but there's a fierceness behind the smile. Is that it?"

Song looked at the boy. "That sounds right to me. I actually have no idea myself, but I thought it sounded good."

Ed carried his plate to the sink and handed it to Max. "Your mother and grandmother will be fine. It's just been a while, that's all." But deep down Ed wondered if things between them would ever be right.

CHAPTER 13

––– •• •• •••– –– • •–• –• ••• •• –– ––– –•• •••

Monday morning dawned crisp and clear, just as the news had said it would. Ed left early for the office, followed by Anna, who had a meeting in the city about her registration. Both of them were gone before the twins had appeared for breakfast. When Fitz offered to put some laundry in, Song had happily grabbed his coat and the dogs and walked the children to school.

Kensy was on high alert, looking for potential paparazzo at every turn, and almost gave one of the elderly ladies who lived in the apartment above the hairdresser on the corner a heart attack when she snuck up behind her and demanded she hand over the camera. The poor woman was just collecting the newspaper from the stoop and had a mug of tea in her hand, which spilled onto the steps.

"Sorry," Kensy had mumbled as she scurried away to rejoin Song and Max.

"Miss Kensington, I really don't think you have anything to worry about," Song said. They crossed Ponsonby Terrace and walked along John Islip Street to the corner of Ponsonby Place, where Derek Grigsby was busy putting the newspaper front pages into the displays outside the shop.

Max didn't want to look. Surely his family would be headline news after the interview last night. As their shadows crossed his path, Derek looked their way.

"Blimey, aren't you lot a sight for sore eyes!" He leapt up and hugged both of the children tightly before giving Song the same treatment. "I thought you was all dead for a while there, then I 'eard you was recoverin' somewhere, but now you're back!" Derek beamed, his gold tooth glinting. "Where are you livin'? Your place is still covered wiv plastic. Don't matter – you've made my day. Song, may I put in a dumplin' order? Unless you want me to wait until you're back in the 'ouse, proper like?"

"Ah, Mr. Derek, it is very good to see you too," Song said, grinning widely. It was the first time they'd seen Derek since their return to London, and Song expected the lad would have many questions.

"I bought some of that smelly stuff you suggested," Derek said. "To attract the ladies. It 'asn't worked yet, though."

Kensy bit back a laugh. "As a member of the female genus, I would suggest that maybe less is more."

"Oh, 'ave I put on a bit too much, do you think?" Derek frowned and sniffed himself.

Kensy nodded, her eyes watering. That was the understatement of the century, but at least the guy was trying.

"You seen the news this mornin'?" Derek motioned at the front page of the *Times*. Max expected to see him and his family. Instead, half of the page was taken up with a story about a huge fire down by the river. It had burned through a whole row of derelict warehouses that had been the subject of a controversial redevelopment. The other half reported a robbery at the British Museum. A precious but ghoulish Mesolithic headdress made from the antlers of a red deer was stolen overnight. Max couldn't help thinking it was a strange thing to take from a museum full of far more attractive antiquities.

It was the same for every other front page – either the fire or the antler headdress or that silly singer who had bitten his girlfriend's dog. There was nothing about them – not in the headlines, at least.

"Did you watch television last night?" Kensy asked the man.

"Wasn't it incredible?" Derek gasped. "I was so pleased when Darcy Pickles and Barry Ladd took out *Dance with Me* – best result ever! Then I switched over to *Killer Cuisine*. That last dessert – it really was almost a killer when Maryam's hair caught on fire, but they put it out and apparently it tasted like heaven."

Kensy breathed a sigh of relief. With a bit of luck, everyone else would have been so busy watching reality television that no one saw the interview.

The children bade farewell to Derek with the promise of a dumpling–candy swap later in the week. As they arrived at school, it seemed like business as usual. Song gave a wave and headed home and the children hurried inside to their lockers.

Misha was busy organizing her books into a neat row when she spotted the twins. "Hey," she said with a smile. "I saw you on the telly last night. It was a great interview. I'm so happy for you all. I'm looking forward to meeting your mum and dad." She gave the twins their second unexpected hug of the morning.

"Thanks. We're hopeful that not too many people watched," Max said nervously.

A few kids walked past and said hello, but no one seemed to be staring or even remotely interested – except for Blair, who ran toward the twins at full speed.

"Oh my gosh!" she exclaimed at the top of her voice. "What was it like being in witness protection for the whole of your lives?"

"Keep it down, Blair, please," Kensy said to the girl. "It wasn't witness protection – our parents just had to get away – but we're back now and everything's fine, so let's not talk about it anymore."

But the girl was not to be deterred. "Your grandmother owns the *Beacon* – she must be *so* rich! Do you live in a mansion?"

Max shook his head. "We're just normal kids who've had some interesting experiences, that's all. It's nothing special and we'd really like to be able to get on with things without becoming some sort of carnival attraction."

"But you're famous now. What was it like at the television studio? Did they give you fancy drinks and delicious food and did someone do your hair and makeup?" The girl went on and on.

"No, it wasn't like that at all," Kensy said, her hands clenched into fists by her side.

"Don't you have lines to learn or somewhere else to be?"

Blair gasped as if she'd just remembered something important. "Oh yes, I said I'd go over my lines with Harriet. You'll have to tell me everything later. Bye!"

Kensy spotted Autumn rushing toward her. One of her hair ribbons was untied and her collar was poking out from her sweater at an awkward angle. "What happened to you?" Kensy asked, her voice tinged with worry. "You look like me in the morning – actually, me most of the time."

Autumn frowned in confusion until Kensy pointed to her ribbon and collar.

"We had a power outage and my alarm didn't go off – my aunt said that we're on the same section of the grid as the docks that burned down. Wasn't it weird all those things happening last night at the same time your interview aired?"

Kensy eyed her friend. "What are you getting at?"

"Ever heard of creating a diversion? Your grandmother is a genius," Autumn said.

Kensy blinked. "You think Granny did all that?"

"Apart from that idiot biting his girlfriend's dog, yes," Autumn said. "Think about it. The docks were due for redevelopment, the builders were starting soon and I'm sure that headdress will turn up again – but it's fun to think someone got into the museum and stole it undetected."

Kensy suddenly remembered that one of the bottles from Mim, Hector and Marisol was called *The Madness Mix*. She'd read more about it and, apparently, it caused the recipient to do strange things that were completely out of character. "I think the dog thing might have been her too – or at least one of her people." Kensy nodded thoughtfully.

"Like I said, the woman is a genius – you're already yesterday's news," Autumn said, quickly retying her ribbon into a perfect bow. "I have to see Madame Verte again. I'll catch you in class!"

"Yep, talk to you then." Kensy waved goodbye and set off to her own appointment with Mr. Richardson. She hurried down the hall to his office, her nerves aflutter, wondering exactly what the teacher had in store.

CHAPTER 14

—·|| ·— ||— —·| —·|—·| ···|| · —·||

"I don't see why I have to wear a skirt." Kensy tugged at the gray A-line garment, which she'd paired with black ankle boots and a teal sweater. At least it wasn't as bad as the dress her mother had made her wear for the television interview.

"You look lovely," Anna said. The woman had also insisted on braiding Kensy's hair and adding a teal ribbon.

"You do too, Mum," Max said, flashing her a smile.

Anna had to admit the floral dress Song had picked out for her was very flattering and terribly pretty and she felt better dressed than she had in years. She just hated that Cordelia had arranged it. "Song has very good taste." The woman grinned and the man gave her a nod from the pull-down seat opposite.

The taxi turned left into a side street off the King's Road in Chelsea and pulled up in front of the restaurant. It had a delicate duck-egg blue facade and signage written in curly script. Max thought it looked upscale but not too posh. There were already quite a few people milling about inside.

"There's Granny," he said, pointing to the window. Sure enough, Cordelia was standing with a woman wearing a red cape and a man in a tartan vest and matching trousers. She was holding a glass of champagne and talking animatedly.

"Please try to enjoy yourselves," Song said. He hopped out and held the door for the family. "I will be back at eight on the dot, and we will be home by quarter past – I can assure you, Mrs. Spencer."

"Thank you, Song," Anna said as she took his hand and stepped out onto the sidewalk.

The children followed their mother up the stairs and inside, where they were greeted by an enthusiastic woman who was checking names off a list. Realizing who she was speaking to, she fired a volley of questions, but Cordelia had spotted her family and glided through the guests to rescue them. She kissed Anna on both cheeks, then kissed and hugged the twins too. Cordelia seemed a lot less prickly than she had last night, which the twins were glad about.

"You all look lovely," she said, and meant it. "Come and meet Lady Adelaide."

She led the way, the crowd parting before them, to Max's amazement. They arrived in front of a tall, thickset woman wearing an emerald dress with a rather daring neckline.

"Lady Adelaide, I'm sure you remember my daughter-in-law, Anna," Cordelia said.

Anna held out her hand, but Lady Adelaide was having none of that. Unlike so many of her aristocratic peers who subscribed to a stiff upper lip and quiet reservation, the woman lunged toward Anna, hugging her fiercely and blubbering about how happy she was to see her. The woman wiped a tear from her eye and held Anna's hands then looked to the children. Kensy hoped that she and Max weren't about to befall the same fate. Lady Adelaide had the sort of enormous bosoms you might end up suffocated between. Fortunately, the woman elected to cup their faces instead, which was still a little too familiar for Kensy's liking.

Lady Adelaide stepped back. "I'm so glad you could come tonight," she gushed. "I know everyone is dying to see you – what a pity Edward wasn't able to attend, but I'm sure we'll catch up with him soon. Dalglish was positively frothing when I told him the news. He's not here either – he's at home with the dogs. Anyway, please make sure you have something to eat. All of the food on the menu is from the book, though I can't say I made it myself this evening." The woman tittered. "Cordelia, you must bring the family to Torridon one weekend." She looked at Kensy and Max. "We have horses and a maze and, when the weather warms up, there's a pool and tennis. You'd love it."

The twins said it sounded great and they looked forward to it. Although neither could tell if the other was just being polite.

"Well done, darlings," Cordelia whispered as Lady Adelaide was called away to greet another flurry of arrivals. "You've charmed the hostess. Now, let's try the food. I have to admit the woman is an amazing cook, and I'm famished. I'd better pop over and buy some books too, given that's the whole point of a launch."

There were waiters wandering about with platters as well as another buffet table at the back of the restaurant. Anna excused herself to go to the bathroom while Max, Kensy and Cordelia headed over to the food. A man in a pin-striped suit and with a strange clump of orange hair stepped into their grandmother's path and began talking to her at high volume. Max looked back to see if they should rescue her, but she gestured for them to save themselves.

A woman wearing cherry lipstick with a brunette bob was standing to the side of the table, taking in the scene, and surreptitiously snapping a few photographs on her phone.

"I can recommend the smoked salmon blinis," she said, noticing that Kensy and Max were eyeing the offerings.

"Thanks," Max said and picked one up, along with a napkin.

His sister went for a homemade sausage roll instead. Kensy dipped it into a bowl of tomato relish and managed to slop some on the white tablecloth as she took a generous bite. A blob landed on the front of her sweater.

The woman smiled. "You're not having much luck there, are you?" She whipped a wet wipe from her handbag and passed it over. "I'm Trelise."

"Kensington," the girl replied, then took another bite of her sausage roll.

The woman's eyes widened in surprise. "Dame Spencer's granddaughter? Of course you are. I saw you on the television last night. You did really well, by the way. But Evan's a sweetheart. I can imagine that's why your grandmother chose him for the interview."

Kensy nodded as she had her mouth full and was still trying to maintain an air of respectability.

"I remember when the accident happened – we were all heartbroken and your grandmother . . . she was incredible. I knew your father a little bit before they went missing. It's wonderful to have him back at the paper. I have to say everyone loves him and he's doing a great job," Trelise said.

Max looked at the woman. She wore a tapered black skirt that skimmed her knees and a cream silk blouse, with towering patent black heels. Elegant jet earrings complemented her look, and her hair and makeup had a professional touch, as if she'd spent the afternoon at the hairdresser and beautician. "Are you a journalist?" the boy asked.

"Social reporter – the hard-hitting stuff." Trelise winked. "But your grandmother gives me a generous allowance so that I can 'fit in,' and my job is great fun." Trelise craned her neck to peer over a trio in front of them. "Is that Theo Richardson with Lady Bosworth?" She spied the man standing in the corner, chatting to a birdlike woman.

"What's he doing here?" Max asked, not meaning for the words to come out quite so loudly.

"Oh, Theo's a regular on the social circuit," Trelise said knowingly. "Though his career seems to have stalled of late. His hosting of the *Christmas Variety Show* was positively awful, as if he wanted to be anywhere but there."

Max wondered if she knew that Theo had taken a job at the school but wasn't going to mention it. Trelise wasn't Pharos – he'd been studying the profiles and photographs of all the staff again yesterday and was confident he could now name and identify every agent at the *Beacon*.

Kensy looked at Theo too. She'd met with him that morning about his plans to help with her quick-change and stealth training. So as not to stoke claims of preferential treatment, he'd added Kensy to the stage crew and suggested they work their extra lessons into the play rehearsals. Max had been surprised to hear that Kensy had joined the production of *Romeo and Juliet*, but was also relieved, given how huffy she'd been over the weekend.

What Mr. Richardson had outlined to her was amazing – she'd definitely beat Max in that part of the review and she couldn't wait to get started, but this afternoon she'd had to stay with the group for the read through at school, just so everyone believed that she really was part of the crew. Tomorrow, when they went to the theater for the first time, he would tell the other kids she was on special duties – and no one would be any the wiser. Kensy couldn't believe what a cool plan it was and how badly she'd misjudged the man. That was something she needed to work on if she was going to truly succeed in the spy game – apparently, first impressions didn't always ring true.

Kensy watched as people greeted Theo like a family member. Lady Adelaide kissed his cheeks three times and several gentlemen shook his hand and hugged him. It was clear he was adored.

Anna reappeared from the bathroom and joined the children. "That's ten minutes I managed to kill," she whispered conspiratorially. "Fifteen minutes to go."

Kensy giggled and gasped in mock dismay. "You look so sweet on the outside, but really, Mum, you are pure evil."

"Wow! Now, there's a scoop!" Trelise exclaimed to no one in particular.

The twins and their mother turned to see a stunning young woman walk through the door. Her lustrous dark hair was so shiny you might have caught your reflection in it at the right angle. Her eyelashes were impossibly long and her skin was like cream. Even from this distance her blue eyes, the color of Ceylonese sapphires, sparkled. Max had never seen anyone so beautiful.

"She must be a model or a movie star," Kensy said. She noticed Theo gazing at the woman. He looked like a little boy whose teddy bear had been missing in the park for days and had suddenly been found.

Trelise nodded. "That's Victoria De la Vega. Made herself a fortune in Hollywood in her teens and twenties, but I recall she had a scurrilous manager who disappeared in strange circumstances along with most of her money. She subsequently ended up in a string of really bad movies, which pretty much cost Victoria her career. She divides her time between Paris and London now, and rumor has it she's a silent partner in a range of business ventures. She never gives interviews and hates the paps with a passion. They avoid her like the plague these days, after several successful lawsuits, but I have it on good authority that she recently had a baby – not that anyone has seen evidence of it and, going by the size of her, you'd never know. I have a reliable source." The woman grinned and arched her left eyebrow.

"She's gorgeous," Max gasped. He blushed, realizing he'd spoken the words out loud when he really just wanted to think them in his head.

"Ooh, Max's got a crush," Kensy teased. "Don't worry, I won't tell Autumn. She'd be devastated."

Max gave his sister a friendly shove.

"I should get some photos," Trelise said. "Wish me luck."

Kensy turned back to the buffet table, this time electing to go for a cheese tart, smoked salmon blini, a bacon croquette and a plate. She had no desire to add to the stain on her sweater or the mess on the tablecloth.

Her grandmother had just grabbed Anna and Max and was introducing them to a woman who appeared to have stepped straight from the pages of a 1960's fashion magazine. Her impossibly tall beehive hairdo was accented by white hoop earrings and a patterned dress that looked as if someone had thrown up on it. Kensy kept her head down, hoping she might escape this round of show-and-tell.

Once she'd filled her plate and reached for a glass of mineral water from a passing waiter, she retreated to a quiet corner to eat, only to find Mr. Richardson there. He was still gazing at Victoria De la Vega. "She's pretty, isn't she?" Kensy said with her mouth full. "Do you know her? I mean, she's an actor, so I suppose you do." Kensy swore under her breath as a morsel of crème fraîche fell on her sweater. She quickly popped it in her mouth and dabbed at the spot with a tissue.

"No, we've never met," Theo replied, unable to tear his gaze away. "Wouldn't know her from a bar of soap."

"Uh-huh." Kensy spat on her sleeve and tried to rub at the spot. She looked up and caught sight of Max cringing at her. Rolling her eyes, she took a bite of her cheese tart. It was delicious. "She keeps looking at you, so maybe you should say hello," Kensy said to Mr. Richardson. She froze when she realized she'd just showered the man's jeans in white flecks of cream cheese and pastry. "Sorry, better go – Granny's giving me the hairy eyeball," the girl mumbled, trying not to open her mouth. Kensy hurried over to the others. Fortunately, the woman with the high hair had just left.

"I was wondering where you'd gone to," Cordelia said.

Kensy handed her empty plate to one of the waiters. "What did I miss?"

Anna looked at her watch and was thrilled to see it had just gone eight. She said goodbye to Cordelia, as did the twins, but all eyes were on Victoria De la Vega, who was also leaving. Although the woman had barely been there for ten minutes, she'd been the center of attention during her short visit. The twins followed their mother to the entrance, where Song was waiting for them. Their cab was parked a little way down the crowded street.

Apparently, some people didn't worry about blocking the road. Victoria hopped into a shiny black Mercedes that was double-parked right outside the restaurant. The twins, Anna and Song set off to their vehicle, but Kensy turned to look back. She was surprised to see Theo walk out of the restaurant and over to the rear passenger window of the Mercedes, which rolled down on his approach. It sounded as if Victoria called out his name.

He shook his head and muttered something unintelligible.

Well, that was strange. Theo just said that he hadn't ever met Victoria De la Vega — that he didn't know her from a bar of soap. Clearly, that wasn't true. But what reason did the man have for lying?

CHAPTER 15

"Honestly, Song, you don't need to walk us to the theater," Kensy insisted. "Autumn's here and so's Carlos and Max. We're *fine*. You said yourself that you need to get dinner started. Isn't Granny coming tonight?"

Song frowned. "Yes, she is, but I have also been tasked with looking after you two. No wonder Confucius says child with strong will is pain in butler's rear end."

The kids burst out laughing.

"Good one, Song," Carlos said.

"Fine," the man relented, "you may walk

to the theater together, but I will be there to collect you in a cab at precisely quarter to six. You will not walk back on your own. Do you understand?"

"Thanks, Song, and I promise we'll try harder not to give you a pain in the bottom. You know, there are creams you can get for that sort of thing." Kensy hugged the man and planted a kiss on his cheek.

"A quarter to six, Miss Kensington, and not one minute later," Song said, still shaking his head as he turned on his heel.

"I wish we had a butler like Song." Carlos grinned. "What am I saying? I wish we had a butler period. He's awesome. I used to think he was a bit crusty when we'd go to Alexandria, but he's actually a really funny guy."

"Who's a funny guy?" Blair said, barging into the middle of the group.

"Never mind," Kensy said.

"Are you disappointed about not getting the part of Juliet?" Autumn asked the girl.

Blair made a face. "No way – have you read the script? She's a total sap. The Nurse is far more challenging, and funny too. She steals the show."

"I'd love to hear her tell Misha that," Carlos whispered to Max, who smiled.

"Anyone got some mints?" Alfie asked when the children arrived at the stage door. Unlike the glorious baroque facade, the stage door at the side of the building was plain and dull and gave no hint as to the architectural delights inside.

"You worried your bad breath will put Misha in a coma when you have to go in for the kiss?" Dante teased.

"What?" Alfie looked horrified. "What kiss?"

Autumn rolled her eyes. "Have you even read the script?"

"Sort of," Alfie said, swallowing hard. "But I didn't see anything about kissing. No offense, Misha, but that's not going to happen, especially not up on stage in front of the whole school and the parents and *Mr. MacGregor*."

Misha rolled her eyes. "I knew you were

the wrong Romeo. It should have been that gorgeous Brian Pemberton in Upper Sixth — pity he didn't try out."

"If he's gorgeous, then I'm the King of England," Alfie said, puffing out his chest. "Let's just take this thing one step at a time, okay?"

Misha grinned. Reverse psychology worked every time.

The children were met by Mr. Richardson, who led them past the dressing rooms to the backstage area, which was vast and dark. With one press of a button, the curtains opened, momentarily blinding the children until their eyes adjusted to the glare of the stage lights. Once they could see past the first few rows, the theater revealed elegant balconies and curves of dark ruby seats. The ornate domed ceiling was breathtaking.

Alfie gulped. "We're not going to fill this place, are we?"

"Probably not, but think about what an incredible experience this is for everyone," Theo said. "We're only here because the theater's between productions and I know the owners. I never got to perform in a place like this until I was a professional actor. Anyway, take this opportunity to go over your lines for the next few minutes and then we'll do a read through. I've just got to do a couple of things first." He motioned for Kensy to follow him. They headed backstage to another huge storage area where there was a bicycle, a helmet and a small black backpack.

Kensy unzipped it and looked inside to find several pairs of glasses, a couple of wigs and various other elements of disguise.

"This is your first target." Theo handed her a piece of paper containing the address, a floor plan and a picture of the object she had to collect. "While there won't be anyone home, you'll still need to get in and disable the alarm. The box is in the entrance hall, though it's papered over, so you'll have to find it. The code's on the page, but don't expect this much information every time. It's likely to get harder. You need to burn the paper once you leave and make sure that no one finds any of the remnants. Bring the object back here and I'll return it later tonight. No one will be any the wiser."

Kensy's spine tingled and her stomach churned. "Sir, I've been thinking . . . What I'm about to do is . . . totally illegal, isn't it?"

Theo nodded. "Why? Are you having second thoughts?"

Kensy let out a deep breath and looked at the man.

"Remember, Kensy, these people are my friends and it's just a training exercise – practice for the real thing when you do need to get into a house and find something or someone. The reason I'm helping you is because a teacher did this for me when I was your age and it became one of my absolute strengths. I've never once come close to being caught. You do want to pass your review, don't you?" Theo said. He grinned and gave her a nudge.

A smile tugged at the corners of Kensy's mouth. "And beat Max," she admitted.

"Even getting to the location and back is great training. You'll be navigating the city better than your brother in no time," Theo said.

"Thanks, Mr. Richardson. I really appreciate it." Kensy jammed the bike helmet on her head before checking the address again and punching it into the navigation app on her phone. She could do this and, what's more, she was going to be great at it.

CHAPTER 16

Kensy jumped into the cab ahead of her brother, a beaming grin on her face.

"Someone has enjoyed herself this afternoon," Song remarked as Max climbed in after her. He was smiling too but didn't seem nearly as ebullient as his sister. "I take it the rehearsal was a success."

"It was good," Max said. "I remembered most of my lines, but it's hard when the others don't come in at the right time. Blair messed up the most, although Alfie was a close second. I thought Mr. Richardson was going to lose it."

"I had the best afternoon!" Kensy was practically fizzing. "It was *amazing*."

"Who knew that sorting props was so exciting?" Max said, looking at his sister. "If that's what you were doing."

Kensy nodded, giggling giddily.

The girl had carried out her mission successfully, delivering a small gold carriage clock to Mr. Richardson well within the allotted time. He had praised her efforts and told her he was going to pop around straight after the rehearsal to return it, so there was no harm done and much had been learned.

At one point during the operation, Kensy's heart was in her mouth when the alarm code didn't work. In her haste, she'd mixed up two numbers. Fortunately, she realized before she set anything off. Mr. Richardson said he had another plan for her tomorrow. She couldn't wait. Apart from leaping across the rooftops of Piccadilly the other night, breaking into that house was quite possibly the most exhilarating thing she'd ever done in her life.

Minutes later, they were home.

"Dinner will be served at seven, so if you have homework, I recommend you get that done now or spend the time studying for your review," Song said as the three entered the kitchen. Something smelled delicious; it was clear that the man had been busy.

"Would you mind taking these to the dining room on your way up?" The man passed Kensy two pairs of silver salt and pepper shakers.

"Sure," the girl replied, and bounded away.

"Your sister is certainly in a very good mood this evening," Song said as Max hung up his coat.

"We should really enjoy it while we can," Max said, rifling through his schoolbag. "You never know when the wind might change."

The two grinned at one another.

Upstairs, Kensy counted the place settings and paused at the two extra ones, wondering who else would be joining them.

Max headed up to his room and rushed through his math homework before turning his attention to Magoo's cipher. He had an idea, and if it worked he would run the code through the enigma machine tomorrow or the next day when there was more time. He felt guilty that he hadn't shared the note with Kensy, even though she'd seen it and decided it was just some nonsensical gibberish. They never really kept secrets from each other and this one felt like a lump of undigested sausage in his stomach. It was just that she had a tendency to jump to wild conclusions. The last thing he wanted was for her to be upset with Magoo for no reason. At least she seemed to be changing her mind about Mr. Richardson.

Kensy was up to her eyeballs in algebra when she was startled by Song's voice. "Please make your way to dinner, children," he said. Kensy looked around the room, perplexed as to when that new technology had been installed and where the sound was coming from. It didn't take her long to work it out. In the middle of the bookshelf was a paperweight — a brass monkey whose eyes were glowing red. Granny Cordelia had one in her office at the *Beacon*.

"The monkey's a nice touch, don't you think?" Max said when the twins met on the landing outside their rooms.

Kensy nodded. "We'll have to ask Granny what their significance is – maybe she just likes monkeys or something? Do you know who else is coming to dinner?"

"No idea," he said, tucking in his shirt. Max had changed out of his school uniform and was wearing a pair of khaki trousers and a long-sleeved checked shirt with boat shoes. Kensy, on the other hand, was still in her uniform and had obviously been lying on her bed, as half her hair had escaped from the plait she'd tied that morning.

The pair galloped downstairs and turned the corner into the back hallway just as Hector and Marisol entered the dining room.

"Grand-mère! Grand-père!" Kensy squealed, running to them. "We didn't know you were coming."

"We did not know either until this afternoon when Cordelia phoned. 'Ow could we say no?" Marisol beamed.

Cordelia walked into the room with Ed, an equally bright smile on her face. "Mim would have loved to be here as well, but she had book club in the village. It was a spy thriller this month, apparently."

"Are you staying with us then?" Kensy asked her grandparents. She pouted when they shook their heads. "But you'll only be here for five minutes," she protested, "and we've got so much to tell you."

"And show you," Max added.

"It is better that we return to Alexandria this evening. But per'aps we can come again soon," Hector said. "Cordelia sent the 'elicopter to pick up some things from Mim and called to ask if we would like to come to London. The journey was far easier than I 'ad imagined, and the access to your 'ouse is quite something."

"Well then, we need to tell you everything now," Kensy said. "We tried some of the potions you sent. That truth serum really works."

"Where did you use it?" Hector asked.

"Tell you later," Kensy whispered, hoping that no one else had heard her confession.

She didn't need her grandmother or Fitz putting two and two together.

Marisol clapped her hands with a youthful glee. "Wonderful," she chuckled. "Actually, your *grand-père* and Mim and I tried *Laughter is the Best Medicine*. Poor Mrs. Thornthwaite wondered if we had some sort of 'ysterical sickness, but then she caught it as well and we laughed until our sides ached."

"You'd better not have any of those concoctions with you at the moment, young lady," Anna said. "We don't need you cackling like a clucky hen through dinner, Kensy."

The family was soon gathered around the long oak table. Ed and Anna sat at either end while Max was between his two grandmothers and Kensy sat opposite, sandwiched by Hector and Fitz. Despite Dame Spencer's entreaties to join them, Song opted to eat in the kitchen as he had to keep a close eye on the dessert. He was testing a new soufflé recipe and wanted to impress the Clements.

There was lots of excited chatter about what was happening at Alexandria, and Kensy and

Max talked about school and their upcoming review. Hector and Marisol said they had watched the interview, and Cordelia reported that there had hardly been any discussion about it at all – thanks to some other big stories that pushed them off the front pages and into the background.

"Did you make all that happen, Granny?" Kensy asked. "Autumn said you're a wizard at creating a diversion."

Cordelia Spencer looked up from her plate, an impish grin on her face. "Let's just say that there were certain opportunities that came about that night, but we certainly had nothing to do with the robbery at the British Museum. That wasn't us."

"But the fire and that silly man biting his girlfriend's dog? I thought that could have been one of Mim's and Grand-mère and Grand-père's potions," Kensy said.

Hector and Marisol looked at each other in surprise.

Cordelia raised her eyebrows. "Let's just be grateful that things played out in our favor."

Conversation soon splintered off around the table with Marisol animatedly telling Cordelia how much she was enjoying the garden at Alexandria, while Hector was speaking quietly to Anna about her forthcoming examinations, asking if there was anything he could help her with. He thought she seemed tense and enquired whether she was sleeping. The dark circles under her eyes were something of a giveaway. As a child, Anna had been prone to grinding her teeth and sometimes had night terrors too. The woman assured them all that she was fine.

Max leaned in as Marisol and Cordelia began chatting about Mim's most recent vegetable successes. "I do that too, Mum," he said quietly. "I woke myself up this morning, chomping away like some demented cow, and I've been having bad dreams lately."

Anna smiled at the boy. "I'm sorry – seems you get it from me."

"My sensitive darlings." Hector looked at his daughter then across at his grandson. "You just 'ave to stop worrying, which I know is easier said than done, considering all this." He waved his hands in the air.

"Has there been any news on those two missing journalists?" Kensy whispered to Fitz.

Unfortunately, she said it a lot louder than she'd intended, because Marisol gasped. "Missing? 'Ave they been taken?"

Cordelia dabbed at her mouth with her napkin, then folded it beside her plate. "It appears so and, no, Kensy, we haven't heard a thing. I wish whoever has them would make contact as it won't be long until their colleagues begin asking questions. And I'm afraid that two has just become three."

"Three!" Max exclaimed. "When did that happen?"

"Trelise Fulton-Jennings hasn't been seen since Lady Adelaide's launch on Monday evening," Cordelia said. "She hasn't been at work and there's no sign of her at home either."

Max shivered. "That's awful."

Kensy frowned. "I talked to her for quite a while. She didn't sound like she was worried about anything."

"I don't believe she was," Cordelia concurred. "Her job at the paper is by far the most fun — she doesn't generally upset people, and none of her stories are particularly hard-hitting."

"Surely there must be something that links the three of them," Max said.

Fitz swallowed his mouthful of food. "We have some leads. Peter is trawling through Trelise's archive as we speak, and he's found some of Harry and Jamila's notebooks too. We're going over everything with a fine-tooth comb."

"I am sorry to 'ear it," Hector said. "And I 'ope that whoever 'as them is not as evil as our captor, nor as determined."

"While we're on the subject of missing people, has Uncle Rupert made any progress finding Dash?" Max asked. They hadn't heard from him since they'd moved back to London.

"Your uncle is on the trail," Ed piped up, "but, true to form, he's keeping his cards close at the moment. I assume we'll hear more when he has something to tell. Anyway, please, none of you are to worry — we'll find them," Ed said, hoping to steer the conversation to lighter topics.

"What about the guys from the boat?" Kensy asked, ignoring her father's lead. "Have you found out who they were?"

Fitz set his knife and fork down on his plate and nodded. "We're pretty sure it was a fellow called Huang and one of his associates. Your father and I took him down for money laundering and murder, among other things, but he recently escaped from a Taiwanese prison and is on the run. We know he was here in London, but he's since fled to America. I have agents on his tail."

"Thanks for telling us," Max said, a terseness in his voice. "Maybe now I'll sleep a little better."

Kensy stared at her brother. "Fitz probably wasn't allowed to say anything. You do know that part of being involved in a covert spy agency is about keeping secrets," she said, a little more forcefully than she'd meant to.

Max knew all about secrets at the moment but wondered if Kensy had anything she was hiding too. It seemed a weird thing for her to say.

"Sorry, mate," Fitz said. "We only got

confirmation this afternoon. I was going to let you know. And you're right, that is one less thing to be worried about."

"For now," Anna added, without looking up from her plate.

An awkward silence descended on the table. For a few minutes, no one said a word, lost as they were in their own thoughts. Max's mind was awhirl – he was thinking about the review, the coded note from Magoo and he was worried about his mother. But Kensy wasn't thinking of any of that. She was hoping that tomorrow's task from Theo would be even more exciting and challenging than today's. She couldn't wait to see what he had in store. Cordelia, on the other hand, was hoping dessert was as tasty as dinner – which she had very much enjoyed so far.

"How have your rehearsals been going, kids?" Fitz asked.

"Great," Kensy said, munching on a crispy baked potato. "Stage crew is awesome."

Max looked up from his plate. He couldn't help feeling that his sister's enthusiasm was somewhat disproportionate, particularly given he'd heard a kid called Lewis complaining about how boring it was.

"I'm surprised you have access to the Victoria for your play," Cordelia said, genuinely impressed. "It's always booked for large-scale productions with professional theater companies, though I must confess I haven't been there in years. Theo must be well connected to have hit on a free spot."

"They're doing some renovations in the foyer," Kensy explained. "So they probably couldn't open for the general public at the moment, anyway. Mr. MacGregor was beside himself about the fact we're performing at such a prestigious venue, but I don't think the rest of the teachers are impressed. I overheard Mrs. Vanden Boom say the rehearsal schedule was manic and she couldn't understand why we had to get the whole thing done in three weeks, especially as we could have used the school hall and spun it out until the last week of term."

"Well, I'm certain it will be an experience

none of you will forget," Cordelia said. "As long as being involved doesn't impact your first reviews. You know, your father and Fitz never failed a single element."

Kensy and Max looked at one another across the table.

"What about Uncle Rupert?" Kensy said.

"That's a story for another time," Cordelia replied.

If the main course was a success, Song's soufflé was a veritable triumph. Marisol said she couldn't remember ever eating one so delicious and the sentiment was shared by the rest of the family. Song was hugely proud of his homemade vanilla ice cream too.

It was just after nine when the happy party broke up. Before their grandparents departed, the twins took Hector and Marisol on a tour of the house, but saved the best till last when they unveiled their workroom in the bowels of the building. Kensy lined up her remote-controlled insect collection to show them. "This is Ferdinand the bee and Frankie the butterfly. I've been working on Roger the dragonfly too, but he's still wingless and a little way off being finished."

Hector inspected each creature closely. He lifted the butterfly to his nose and sniffed. "Is that Chanel No. 5?" he asked.

Anna frowned at her daughter, realizing that's why she couldn't locate her atomizer this morning.

Kensy's cheeks turned red. "Just a tiny bit – I was trying to neutralize the truth serum. I'll buy you a new bottle when I earn some money," she promised.

"When you're about eighteen," Fitz teased. "Or perhaps make that twenty-five, by the time you finish university."

"You might want to test this one in your butterfly at some point." Marisol picked up the bottle labeled *On the Nose*. "But only if you are using it on a sworn enemy."

"We thought that one probably had a horrible smell," Max said.

"That would be an understatement," Hector replied with a grin. "It is a form of repellent that will make your enemy smell like a sewer in one sharp spray. It lasts for twenty-four hours and guarantees no one will want to go near them. In fact, they will not want to be near themselves. I tell you, Mim is a bad influence – this one was her suggestion."

The twins giggled. Kensy was already hatching a plan to test it on Blair if the girl infiltrated HQ again.

The group bade farewell as Song helped Cordelia into her coat and she wound a scarf around her neck. The children hugged their grandparents with promises of catching up on the weekend via video link to Alexandria. Kensy wanted to see if her grandfather could help her with another project in the workroom, and Max had been surprised to learn that one of his *grand-mère*'s favorite pursuits was solving puzzles and codes. Given she knew nothing about Mr. MacGregor, he wondered if it would be a good idea to get her to help him with the cipher – she would be none the wiser about who had created it.

CHAPTER 17

— ·—· ·· —·—· —·— ·—· —· —··
— ·—· ·— ·——· ···

Max executed a sweeper kick, which saw Kensy land flat on her back on the mat.

"Gotcha!" The boy leapt up, though he wasn't counting on his sister's resolve. She rolled over and grabbed his left ankle, sending him crashing to the floor.

"Excellent move, Miss Kensington," Song said. "Tag me in, Master Maxim."

Kensy giggled. "Are you serious?"

"He's wearing a tracksuit, Kensy," Max said. "Have you ever seen Song in activewear before? And, look, he's even taken off his shoes. He's serious."

Kensy bit her lip. Her brother was right. Song was usually dressed in a tuxedo at her grandmother's estate in Alexandria, or smart-casual wear in the city. He did surprise them on occasion, like the other night, when he donned his ninja stealth suit for their parkour review, and this looked like another one of those times. How had she not noticed? With the recent attack and their upcoming review, her mind was all over the place these days. But it wasn't just that. She couldn't stop thinking about the next challenge Theo would present her with.

Kensy had been disappointed to find that the play rehearsals on Wednesday and Thursday were moved to the school hall, as lots of the cast had sports training beforehand and there was no way Mr. Nutting was letting them off. Because of this last-minute change, she and the rest of the stage crew weren't required, which gave her more time to study, but what she really wanted was extra on-the-ground experience. Friday's exercise had been a doddle compared to Tuesday. She'd taken a pair of earrings from a ground-floor apartment in Knightsbridge. The back door was unlocked and the earrings were sitting on a dressing table for all the world to see. Theo had been very pleased, but Kensy was getting bored. She requested that he up the ante next time.

"It's okay, Song, I'll go easy on you," Kensy said with a grin.

"Thank you, Miss Kensington – your care is most appreciated," the man said before he squared up to the girl.

Kensy landed a blow on his right shoulder then a kick to his left thigh. Max was watching closely. Song was up to something; he just wasn't sure what it was yet.

"Come on, Song, you can do better than that," Kensy taunted. "Fitz never lets me off lightly and neither does Max – although I usually have *him* begging for mercy."

And with that invitation in place, Song raised his left leg and, with barely a move, flicked his big toe into Kensy's stomach, sending her flying through the air.

"Whoa!" Max exclaimed. "How did you do that?"

Kensy was back on her feet in a flash. She charged at the man, who did little else but hold up his right forefinger and press it to the middle of her forehead, keeping her completely at bay. Kensy tried to lift her arms but they wouldn't work and, no matter how much force she exerted, grunting and heaving, she couldn't repel him. In the end, Kensy gave up and waited until Song released her from his hold.

"You need to teach us that – and preferably today." Kensy rolled her neck and shoulders. Her eyes glinted and a mischievous grin spread across her face. "I hope combat's part of our review. I can't wait to use that on Mr. Nutting. He'll freak! Unless every agent is *au fait* with the technique . . ."

Song smiled. "I do not believe so."

They spent the next hour working with Song and couldn't believe the things he knew.

But he stopped short of his hypnotizing trick, deciding to save that for another time.

"One of these days I'm going to be able to take *you* down with a single finger," Kensy said when they called it a day.

The butler bowed and reached for his glasses on the shelf. "I am counting on it, Miss Kensington."

The children hurried upstairs to have a shower and get changed. They had to be at the theater in an hour. Song did the same but in half the time.

Anna had left that morning to attend a three-day course at Durham University, while Ed had gone with Fitz and Peter to Harry Stokes's apartment to see if they might have missed anything. They were heading to Jamila's place afterward and then to Trelise's too. They'd spent the morning in the kitchen at Ponsonby Terrace, going through the archives of Harry, Jamila and Trelise's past stories to see if there were any connections between the three journalists beyond the fact that they were all employees at the paper. If only the kidnappers would make some demands, then at least they'd know what they were up against. Given it was Sunday, and Harry and Jamila had been missing for over a week now, they were beginning to get desperate.

The twins barreled into the kitchen.

"Do we have time to eat?" Kensy asked, sitting at the kitchen table in front of the toasted ham-and-cheese sandwich Song had prepared for her.

Max scooted in opposite.

"Yes. I will take you to the theater in a taxi," the man said.

Max was going to object and say they were happy to walk, but it was probably better they did it Song's way. That would keep their parents happy too. The boy took a bite and glanced at a summary matrix of stories and information pertaining to each of the missing journalists that he'd brought downstairs with him. He was working on the case whenever he had a minute, which wasn't as often as he would have liked.

"Are they any closer to finding them?" he asked, nodding at the papers on the table.

His father and the others had left their files behind too.

Song shook his head. "To the best of my knowledge the answer is no. I would say that it is very strange for someone to disappear without leaving a single trace, but then we know what happened to your grandparents. There are clever people who are able to do despicable things and we just have to hope that the journalists have not befallen a similar fate."

"Do you think Dash could have anything to do with it?" Kensy asked, taking a slurp of her chocolate milkshake. "We know he's capable of anything, and he probably wants revenge on Granny for us finding out about his evil empire."

But something had caught Max's eye on the page. It was a reference to an underworld gang of thieves thought to be operating in London and Europe who were involved in money laundering and theft-to-order. Harry Stokes had been working on the story but was yet to identify the kingpins behind it all. Max scanned to the piece Jamila had been writing before she disappeared. It was about a company that had recently gone bankrupt, leaving hundreds of investors not only stone broke but personally broken. She was still to find out who was behind the business that seemed to have no end of phony directors. Trelise Fulton-Jennings's last story had been about Lady Adelaide's book launch and was published the day she disappeared. She must have sent it in straight after the event.

Max opened another file and thumbed through clippings and photos. There were several of Victoria De la Vega at the launch and other events and some of Theo Richardson. It looked like Trelise was a little obsessed with both of them.

"Max, do you think it's Dash who's kidnapped the journalists?" Kensy said again, annoyed that her brother was ignoring her.

Max shook his head. "Dad and Fitz said that Uncle Rupert was certain he's hiding somewhere in America, and I can't see why he'd kidnap journalists who have nothing to do with him – unless it's all some kind of perverse payback for us finding Grand-mère and Grand-père."

"That's what I just said," Kensy sighed. "You never listen to me."

When the children finished their sandwiches, Song handed them each a lunch box containing their afternoon tea. The butler grabbed his coat and they hurried downstairs then caught the elevator to the basement apartment in John Islip Street, where a taxi was waiting for them.

CHAPTER 18

—·—· ·—·· ——— ··· · —·—· ·— ·—·· ·—··

"Places, everyone!" Mr. Richardson clapped his hands and looked out at the cast and crew. "Miss Ziegler, would you mind coming up here and keeping a check on the cast to ensure no one misses their cue?"

A brilliant smile flashed across the young math teacher's face as she leapt up, eager to help. Everyone moved off – the actors to their places and the stage crew to various jobs, from lighting and sound to props and wardrobe. Kensy didn't know quite what to do and was relieved when Mr. Richardson called her over and led the way to the loading dock.

"Your next assignment," he said, handing her a folded piece of paper. "And I suggest you wear this." He reached around the back of a door and passed her a dark overcoat.

Kensy shrugged it on and quickly unfolded the page, barely able to contain her excitement. The property was located on Tregunter Road, South Kensington, and it seemed she had to procure some fancy-looking egg. She peered at the image of it.

"Are you sure you want *that*?" Kensy asked. It looked extremely fragile.

Theo nodded. "Yes, that's exactly what you *have* to get. And be careful. It's worth . . . being careful."

Kensy was pretty sure he was about to say "worth a fortune" but she was kind of glad he didn't. She was already feeling the pressure.

"The bike's outside," Theo said, flashing her a smile. "And don't forget to have fun. You're doing great, Kensy – brilliantly, in fact. Just don't get caught."

Kensy's chest puffed out and she felt as if her feet were about to lift off the ground. She'd really misjudged Mr. Richardson. He was amazing.

Outside, Kensy jammed the helmet on her head and tucked the paper into her jacket, then pedaled off into the Sunday afternoon traffic. She could feel her heart racing at the thought of what was to come. These exercises were pure exhilaration. Now she knew what people meant when they said things like skydiving had turned them into adrenaline junkies. Except that her version was breaking into houses and borrowing things. It technically wasn't stealing if it was going to be returned. She arrived at the location in just under twenty minutes and stood on the other side of the road, scoping out the house. It was an end-of-terrace house with an alley between it and where another row of houses began.

Kensy wheeled her bike down the alley and left it hidden behind a bush, then reached into her backpack and donned a black wig and beanie. She completed the outfit with dark sunglasses.

There were no lights on inside the house as far as she could tell. Mr. Richardson had said that the owners weren't there, but she still had to find a way inside and disable the alarm.

There was a metal gate that opened into a large garden at the rear of the house. It was locked. Kensy wondered if she should try to pick it or just climb over the wall. She glanced up the lane to the road and saw a man in a bowler hat and black coat walking a brindle-colored whippet. The dog stopped to do its business on the small patch of lawn and she could see the fellow looking her way. Kensy stared back at him. She thought he seemed embarrassed and he hurriedly picked up the dog's droppings in a plastic bag and rushed away.

Kensy plucked her regulation school hair clip from under her wig and, seconds later, had the gate unlocked. She also sprayed the rusty hinges with lubricant from a tiny perfume atomizer. She didn't want the gate squeaking and attracting unnecessary attention.

Considering the state of the hedges and the way the weeds were competing for space, the garden hadn't been tended for some time – maybe even since last summer. Kensy scanned the building. According to the floor plan, there was an alarm pad located just inside the back door.

She crept up the stairs and examined the door lock. This one would require two pins. She knelt down and almost had it a couple of times. Trouble was, the spindle wouldn't turn. But Kensy wasn't about to give up. She removed her glasses and tried again. There was a click and another click and – *voilà!* – the lock was conquered. She scampered inside and disabled the alarm, having recited the code in her head at least twenty times on the way over. She wasn't going to make the same mistake twice.

Kensy had also memorized the internal layout of the house and the position of the egg. It was on a side table in the front sitting room, beside a couch.

It was clear no one had been in the house for a while – the air was musty, and chilly too. Considering the furnishings and artwork, whoever lived there could probably afford to retreat somewhere warm and sunny for the winter.

Kensy walked through the modern black kitchen and down the hallway. The sitting room was off to the left. She spotted the egg and gasped. It was mesmerizing. Standing on three gold legs, the pink shell was smattered with pearls that looked like they were attached to delicate gold stems with green leaves beneath them – it was obviously designed to look like lily of the valley. There was a tiny jewel-encrusted crown on the top.

"Wow," Kensy murmured, and began to search for its case. The egg was definitely in peril without it, particularly as she was riding a bicycle – one wrong move meant potential disaster. The information she had said there would be a box, but where she'd find it was a complete mystery. Kensy scoured the room. There were lots of other treasures, but nothing suited her purpose. She opened a cabinet beside the fireplace and, thankfully, there it was. A gorgeous red velvet package with the word "Fabergé" on the side. That had to be it. Kensy quickly removed it and, as gently as she could, placed the fragile object snugly inside and put it into her backpack. She was about to leave when she heard footsteps on the stoop and a key turn in the front door.

"It's so good to be home, Charles," a woman said loudly in a posh English accent. "I don't think I could have coped with another minute of Trudy Brocade and her stories. She does go on."

"It's freezing in here, Prunella," a man complained. "I thought you were going to have Marta air the house and make sure that the heating was on for our return."

For a moment Kensy felt as frozen as the house. She had to think fast and move faster. Not thirty seconds later, a siren blared, providing Kensy with the kick start she needed.

"Shut it off, woman," the man yelled. Fortunately, the noise ceased almost immediately.

Kensy crept into the hallway and was now pressed into an alcove beside a tall display cabinet. She could see the woman's reflection in the mirror above the fireplace and she was heading her way – until she turned into the sitting room and Kensy made a dash for the kitchen. The woman wasn't still for long and was complaining loudly about how she'd just close everything up until the furnace kicked in. Kensy heard the *clackety-clack* of high heels on the marble floor and ducked down behind the island.

"Charles," the woman shouted, "how do I turn the heating on again?"

"It's inside the pantry, dear," he called back. It sounded as if he was upstairs.

Kensy swallowed hard. Her heart felt as if it was about to beat right through her chest. She was surprised the woman couldn't hear it. A phone beeped. Kensy peered out from her hiding spot and saw the woman in full view. She was probably in her late seventies or early eighties, dressed in a pale-blue twinset and pearls, with elegant tapered trousers and stilettos.

"Oh, darling Theo," she said, and chuckled to herself.

"What's that, dear?" The man walked into the room. He was wearing a white shirt and red cravat and had a thatch of silver and black hair. Kensy thought he looked a bit like a badger.

"Theo might pop over to see us this evening. Dear boy," the woman said. "He makes me feel young again."

Kensy grinned. Mr. Richardson's job was going to be a lot easier than hers if he just had to walk through the front door and get the egg back into place without them noticing. Kensy still had to find a way to leave. As the man walked to the sink to fill the kettle, she seized her chance and somersaulted to the other side of the island.

"Did you say something, dear?" the woman asked, walking out of the pantry with a packet of shortbread in her hand.

"Not a word," he replied as he heaped loose-leaf tea into a silver pot and procured two china mugs from a drawer.

"Did you contact the security company?" she asked him.

"Drat it, no," he said. "I'll call them now." He walked away down the hall.

"Charles, I've got my phone here," Prunella shouted after him, but the man didn't return.

This was Kensy's chance. She waited until Prunella had her back turned and ran to the door. But she wasn't fast enough. Just as she'd reached the other side and was about to flee into the yard, the woman spotted her.

"Here they are now, Charles," the woman called, and opened the back door. "You don't usually come this way, do you?"

Kensy pulled her beanie lower and turned around at the bottom of the steps. "Erm, just checking the rear perimeter, madam," she replied, lowering her voice by three registers, the way Theo had taught them.

"Oh good," the woman said, squinting. "Sorry, I set off the alarm. Can't see a thing without my glasses – I lost them yesterday."

The doorbell proved to be Kensy's savior. Charles went to open it. "Security's here," he bellowed.

Prunella spun around in confusion. When she turned back to ask who it was exactly that she was speaking to, Kensy was gone.

CHAPTER 19

▪━━ ▪▪▪▪ ▪ ▪━━▪ ▪ ▪▪━▪ ━━━ ▪━▪

▪━ ▪━▪ ━ ━ ▪▪▪▪ ━━━ ▪▪━ ━━▪▪━

━▪━ ▪ ━▪ ▪▪▪ ▪▪ ━▪ ━━▪ ━ ━━━ ━▪ ▪▪━━▪▪

Kensy rode back to the theater feeling as if she could fly. She toyed with the idea of suggesting that her next mission involve some climbing – a second- or third-floor apartment, perhaps. There was no way she was going to fail the stealth and quick-change sections of the review now. She loved that she'd had to think on her feet – granted there was a bit of luck this time – but she hadn't panicked and that was a huge part of being a successful agent. A twinge of guilt tugged at her insides. She still hadn't shared what she was up to with her brother. They never kept secrets from one another. But it was only until the review and then she'd tell him everything. Besides, he got a part in the play and she didn't – and it was Mr. Richardson who suggested the additional training.

Kensy arrived back at the theater an hour before rehearsal was due to finish, which was slightly problematic as she didn't have a job and wasn't keen to leave the egg unattended either. Maybe she could just squirrel herself away in one of the back rooms and wait until the cast was on a break. She could hear Mr. Richardson shouting directions and he didn't sound happy.

She wandered down a hallway to the end and found a locked door. Hardly a challenge, Kensy thought to herself. With her trusty hair clip in hand, she had that sorted in less than a minute. It felt good to be proficient at something. Kensy stepped inside the room and looked around. It was full of interesting curiosities and she wondered whether it was an old props store. There were lamps, rugs, vases and even a taxidermy brown bear.

Kensy spied a carriage clock like the one she'd taken from the Chelsea address – but that couldn't be right because Mr. Richardson said he'd returned it. She ferreted through the shelves and was surprised to find several jewelry boxes containing beautiful earrings and pendants as well as a framed stamp, a coin collection and a ceramic toilet bowl covered with a pattern of blue and white flowers. There were paintings too, and a creepy assortment of what looked like teeth displayed in a frame. Kensy gagged at the sight of them. Why a theater would need such odd and tiny props was beyond her. She trawled the room and spied a computer attached to a 3-D printer, but it was what she found programmed into it that was most curious. Kensy peered at the screen and began to connect the dots. "You can't be serious!" she whispered.

The roller-shutter door to the loading dock flew up, flooding the room with light. She ducked down out of sight behind one of the racks and held her breath. After what she'd just seen, Kensy had a feeling this was the last place she wanted to be found.

"The girl is doing well," a man said in a thick French accent. "That clock she brought the other day is one of a kind."

"*Oui,*" another man replied.

"Along with the Fabergé, it will be a very good payday for us," the first man said.

Kensy's stomach flipped. She peered through a gap in the shelving. There was nothing remarkable about either of them. They were just two regular guys of the same height and build, dressed in black.

"Let's get moving. We need to pack the truck," one man said. "There are a couple of deliveries close by. We can come back for the rest later."

Kensy sat back against the shelf, her mind racing. What on earth had she done?

* * *

"Well, thank goodness someone is up to par. That was brilliant, Misha." Mr. Richardson clapped loudly as the scene ended. "Okay, everyone, take ten – except you, Alfie. We need to discuss your kissing technique."

The boy's groan was met with a volley of laughter from the rest of the cast.

Poor Alfie had gone to kiss Misha in the balcony scene but pulled away at the last second. Unfortunately, it was obvious that he hadn't even grazed her cheek, and when he was supposed to do it for a second time, he just stared at the girl blankly and shook his head.

"Where's Kensy?" Autumn asked Max, as he and Carlos sat down in the front row to eat their afternoon tea.

"I don't know. I haven't seen her since we got here. But whatever she's been doing, apparently she loves being part of the stage crew. Almost made me wish I'd gone for that instead of a role in the play," Max said. "Cupcake?"

Autumn plucked one from the container then decided to try to find her friend. She walked into the wings and backstage, following a passageway containing dressing rooms and other storage areas.

"There you are." Autumn spotted Kensy coming out of a doorway at the end of the hall. The girl's face was ashen. "Are you all right? You look like you've seen a ghost."

Kensy shook her head. "I'm fine. Just been organizing some props."

But the truth was, Kensy was far from fine. If her hunch was correct, there was much more to Mr. Richardson's stealth training than she'd ever imagined.

Autumn offered Kensy the last bite of her cupcake, but the girl refused. She felt sick to her stomach. How could she have been *so* naïve? Then again, Mr. Richardson had been very convincing. He had indeed been returning the goods – it's just that they were fakes, created by the 3-D printer, and the real things were being delivered elsewhere.

"I can tell you're lying to me," Autumn said.

"No, you can't," Kensy scoffed.

"Yes, I can. Something's up and I wish you'd trust me enough to tell me. I mean, I didn't tell anyone you were in Sydney – not even Carlos, and I knew that he knew, and he knew that I knew, but we still didn't blab."

Kensy hesitated. Apart from Max, she'd never been so close to anyone her own age before. "Okay, come with me, but this stays between us," she said. "I haven't said a word to Max and I don't want him finding out. It's too awful for words."

Autumn nodded. They didn't have long because she was in the scene after the next one and the cast was due back on stage in less than five minutes. Kensy pulled her hair clip from her pocket and fiddled with the lock. Within a few seconds they were in the room at the back of the theater. She turned on the light.

Autumn frowned. "What are we looking at exactly?"

Kensy reached into her backpack and

pulled out the box containing the egg. She opened it and held it up for Autumn to see.

The girl's frown lines deepened. "I'm not following . . . What is this?"

"It's a Fabergé egg," Kensy said, handing the girl the package.

Autumn shook her head. "You're going to have to be more specific. I don't speak egg very well."

"That means it came from the Fabergé jewelers in Russia and it's probably worth at least a few million pounds. Maybe more."

Autumn flinched and almost dropped it. "You can have it back," she said, thrusting it into Kensy's hands. "So, why do you have a multimillion-pound egg in your backpack?"

"I stole it," Kensy replied. "And these earrings too." She opened the velvet box to reveal the Cartier diamond drops she'd taken from the house in Kensington earlier in the week.

Autumn's jaw fell open. "Why would you do that?"

"Because Mr. Richardson said that he was

helping me with my stealth and quick-change skills in real-life situations. He said he'd return the goods straightaway and said he'd learned his best tricks when someone had given him the same training when he was young. I thought there was no harm in it and I really wanted to beat Max at something. But now I suspect Mr. Richardson is part of a gang of thieves and he duped me into helping them," Kensy said.

"Whoa!" Autumn's eyes widened. "Are you serious?"

Kensy nodded. She felt as if she might throw up. So much for passing her review. And as for her ability to make good judgements about people, well, that was a big fat fail too. Her gut instinct about the man had been right – it was her ego that needed reining in.

"What are you going to do?" Autumn asked.

Kensy's shoulders sagged. "Maybe if we knew who else was involved we could take it to Granny and bust the ring wide open, but at the moment I don't know enough. She'll disown me for being such a fool."

"I have to get back for my scene or someone will come looking and the last thing we need is for Mr. Richardson to find us in here," Autumn said.

Kensy agreed. She had to come up with a plan – or else she might as well resign from Pharos right now.

The girls were about to leave when the roller shutter screeched opened again. Kensy grabbed Autumn and they ducked down behind some sort of dinosaur skeleton.

It was the same men who had been there before. This time they spoke to each other in French and one of them wanted to know if the egg had arrived. He then said something about a drop-off in Highgate.

"We have to get out of here," Autumn whispered.

"Or," Kensy said slowly, "we could go with them and find out where they're taking the stuff. They were here before, so the deliveries must be local. He just said Highgate – that's not far."

Autumn hesitated. "I need to head back

to the rehearsal and it's too dangerous for you to go on your own."

"I'll be fine – at least then I can see what they're up to. Trust me," Kensy said. "I'll be back before you know it. Besides, I've already broken into three houses in the past week and I haven't been caught. Give my backpack to Mr. Richardson, okay? Tell him I wasn't feeling well."

Autumn didn't like this idea one bit, but she took the bag and gave Kensy a hug. Kensy waited until the men were rummaging about in the cupboard in the far corner then made her move, scurrying across the floor and leaping into the van, where she hid behind a bulky piece of furniture. Her heart was pounding. Autumn peered through a gap in the dinosaur ribs. She could feel the perspiration trickling down her temples and wiped it away.

The men located what they were looking for and one of them growled something in French.

"What about the Highgate delivery?" the other man asked.

"It can wait until tomorrow," his partner replied, and slammed the van doors shut. He secured them with a heavy chain and padlock. "I 'ave 'ad a call. Tonight we go to Rue las Cases. From there we will be guided by the hand of God to our biggest payday yet."

Autumn racked her brain; she had to think fast. Her French was rusty, but it certainly didn't sound as if Kensy was going to be back anytime soon.

CHAPTER 20

--- . .... . -- .. --
--- .... .. - - .---

Autumn returned to the stage, trembling. Somehow, even with her mind reeling from what had just happened, she managed to keep her composure for the rest of the rehearsal. When at last Theo called an end to the day, Autumn scurried over to Max, who was joking around with Carlos.

"M-Max, I need to speak to you," Autumn stuttered, worrying the hem of her black hoodie.

"Hey, are you okay?" the boy asked. "You look kind of peaky."

Autumn flushed. How was she supposed to tell him his sister had been kidnapped by thieves? "I–I'm all right. It's actually Ke–"

"No, you look really pale," Carlos insisted. He took a step backward. "You don't have gastro, do you?"

"I'm perfectly healthy, thank you very much," Autumn said irritably. "And if I did have gastro, I'd have something in my bag to cure it instantly. You know I'm always prepared for anything." Although, come to think of it, she hadn't been ready for what had happened backstage.

"Did you find Kensy?" Max asked. "We'd better hurry up because Song will be waiting. With everything that's been going on lately, he's being super overprotective."

Autumn glanced around, then pulled the boy aside. "Kensy is on her way to Paris," she whispered.

Max broke into a grin. "What? Did she fancy a late-night trip to the Eiffel Tower?"

Carlos laughed, but the expression on Autumn's face told them this was no joke.

"You're serious?" Max said.

"Okay, here's the thing." Autumn took a deep breath. "Kensy hasn't been helping with the stage crew; she's been doing extra training activities set by Mr. Richardson. This afternoon she realized that she's actually been stealing some very expensive pieces of art and jewelry from private homes – belonging to his friends, apparently – and, contrary to Theo claiming to return the items, Kensy thinks he's been using a 3-D printer to make copies. It looks as though he's been replacing the real things with fakes and making a profit."

The boys looked over at their drama teacher, who was giving Alfie further direction on how to appear as if he was in love, because gagging at the sight of Juliet wasn't going to work at all. Could it be true? Or was this just another one of Kensy's flights of fancy? A thought niggled its way into Max's consciousness.

"When we attended Lady Adelaide's book launch the other night, Mr. Richardson was there too," the boy said, deep in thought.

"He seemed to know everyone, and they all adored him. Kensy wouldn't have any reason to doubt his story . . . No wonder she changed her tune about him so quickly." Max shook his head. "I thought it was weird."

Autumn relayed how Kensy had hidden in the van, expecting to witness a drop-off in Highgate, when in reality she was locked in for a trip to Paris. Max was now the same color as Autumn.

"Do you think those guys are dangerous?" Carlos's features clouded with concern.

"I'll call her," Max said. "Please tell me she had her phone."

Autumn and Carlos stared at him as if he'd lost his mind. "What's the first rule of communication on a mission?" Carlos asked.

"It's not a mission — it's a missing Kensy," Max said, his voice rising. "Isn't it?"

"Your sister is captive in a van heading for Paris and there are stolen goods involved — some that she was responsible for stealing. I'd hazard that puts this squarely in the range of a mission," Carlos said.

"Exactly. Dame Spencer doesn't trust the networks, remember?" Autumn said. "And there's another robbery planned for tonight — one of the men said that it was their biggest payday yet."

The boys turned to her expectantly.

"Well, what is it?" Max asked.

Autumn shrugged helplessly. "All he said was that they would be guided by the hand of God — whatever that's supposed to mean."

"Could be a church?" Carlos said. "Maybe they're planning to steal the treasures of Notre Dame — they've all been moved since the fire. I read something about them being stored in the vault at the Louvre and the Hotel De Ville."

"Could the hand of God be a painting?" Max said.

"I'm on it." Autumn pulled out her phone and grinned when she spotted the surprise on Max's face. "It's okay — I'm just doing some research, not calling anyone."

"Was Kensy wearing her watch?" Max

knew it would be nothing short of miraculous if she was. Now that their parents were back, Kensy didn't see the need to wear it all the time. Even before that, she forgot as often as she remembered, but he was crossing his fingers. At least then he could send her a message and she could let them know where she was. Unfortunately, he'd left his at home today too. He'd forgotten to put it back on.

"I think so," Autumn said. "She might have needed it, given what she was up to. If we go to St. Pancras, we can get a train and be in Paris before Kensy arrives. But we need to go via your house and collect your watch and passport."

"What about yo⟨ ⟩ passports?" Max said.

His friends grinned. "It's protocol to have one on us at all times," Carlos said, whipping his out.

Max grimaced. "We must have missed that lesson. I think we should tell Song. He can help us. Mum's away and Dad's out with Fitz on the hunt for the missing journalists; Song will know what to do."

"What missing journalists?" Autumn asked, her eyes wide. "From the *Beacon*?"

Max nodded. "I'll fill you in later. Let's –"

Mr. Richardson called to them from down the hall. "Guys, have you seen Kensy?"

"She wasn't feeling well, sir, but she said to give you this." Autumn passed him the backpack. "She said it contains the props you'd asked her to sort out for repairs."

Theo nodded and took the bag. "Oh, yes, of course. Tell her I hope she's feeling better soon . . . You didn't see what was in there, did you?"

"No, Kensy just gave it to me as she was leaving," Autumn lied, plastering a smile across her face.

"Brilliant. Lots of surprises in here. See you all tomorrow," Theo said. As he walked off, his phone rang.

Max and Carlos headed out the stage door, but Autumn chose to hang back in the shadows.

"I've done everything you've asked," Theo hissed into his phone. "When will you let me see her?" Autumn was surprised to hear the anguish in his voice. "She's my *daughter*. You can't keep her hidden from me forever. I'll be there tonight and don't you even think about going anywhere."

He hung up and Autumn scurried outside to find her friends. Theo Richardson was a man of mystery, that was for sure. He was also a Pharos agent and had taken an oath. Autumn had no idea what happened to rogues, but she didn't imagine Dame Spencer dealt with them kindly.

Max and Carlos were standing outside, looking up and down the street. "That's weird. Song should be here. Unless something's wrong," Max said. He suddenly had a horrible feeling, but at least there were no plumes of smoke in the sky coming from the direction of their house this time.

Max called the man's phone and was surprised when it went straight to voice mail. His father didn't pick up either and neither did Fitz. There was no point calling his mother; she was in Durham and couldn't do anything even if she wanted to. It would only worry her. That left Granny, who picked up on the second ring.

"Hello, darling, it's a little hard to hear, I'm afraid," she shouted above a blur of white noise. "Unexpected trip home. I've taken Song with me. Mrs. Thornthwaite's been struck down with the flu and Sidney's away for the weekend. Song says he left a message with Fitz to pick you and Kensy up from the theater. Is he there?"

Max's heart sank. "All fine, Granny."

"What's that? Sorry, darling, we're in the helicopter – I can't hear you very well. If you're all okay, I'll speak to you later," Cordelia said, and the line went dead.

"Looks like we're on our own," Max said. "You'd better tell your parents and your aunt that you're spending the night at my place."

The children hailed a cab and not ten minutes later were bundling into the basement apartment in John Islip Street.

"Seriously?" Carlos gasped, as they rode the elevator to number thirteen. "This is . . . new."

Autumn laughed. "That's one word for it."

"Wait until you see the rest of the place," Max said, grinning. They stepped inside to find no one home. Song had left instructions on the counter for Fitz as to what he had planned for dinner. "I'll get my things. Help yourselves to whatever's in the fridge – there's also cake and fruit in the pantry." He grabbed his black hoodie and three black beanies, which he thought might come in handy.

Max was gone no more than five minutes, which had left very little time for Carlos and Autumn to explore the new and improved house. Autumn hadn't even made it past the kitchen, caught up as she was in the contents of a Pharos file on the missing journalists that had been left on the counter. She sifted through the notes and photos until something caused her to pause. She tucked the picture into her jacket pocket. There was something else too: an amount scribbled on the paper with an awful lot of zeroes.

Max led Carlos and Autumn to the workshop downstairs, opening the door with his palm print.

Carlos's eyebrows jumped up as they stepped inside. "You've been holding out on us. How come you didn't tell me about this place?"

"I guess we've been busy and there's so much else going on at school that I just . . . forgot. Sorry. Granny had it built specially." Max surveyed the room for anything that could prove useful on their mission. He scooped up the bottles Hector and Marisol had sent before his eyes fell upon Kensy's collection of remote-controlled bugs. She'd kill him if they got damaged, but it was worth the risk. He placed them carefully into his backpack, along with two pairs of glasses and the remote control. To the stash, he added a Pharos-issue Swiss Army knife, which contained far more interesting features than the standard device: the tape measure zip line they'd used on the top of the building the other night and a spare pair of lasso shoelaces.

"Should we try to send Kensy a message?" Carlos asked.

Max shook his head. "I'll do it once we're on the train. Come on, we need to find a taxi."

CHAPTER 21

— ·· · ··· — ·· —·· — — ·· —— —·
·—·· ·— ·—· ·· ···

"Hello," Autumn said to the pointy-looking woman behind the ticket counter. "I'd like to purchase three tickets to Paris, please, for the five-oh-one service?"

The woman twitched and peered over her reading glasses. "How old are you? Children under the age of twelve aren't allowed to travel on the Eurostar without an adult."

"Um . . ." Autumn quickly glanced around. She spotted an older man with a friendly face sipping from a takeaway cup. She smiled at him and gave a wave, hoping he'd do the same.

Fortunately, he raised his gloved hand. "That's my *grand-père*. He doesn't speak English, I'm afraid, and we're running awfully late – our rehearsal at the theater went over time and, if we don't get this train, we'll be in terrible trouble from Maman," she babbled.

A fellow behind them yelled for the woman to hurry up. Autumn pulled out her wallet and handed over the money in exchange for the tickets. In a bizarre stroke of luck, the woman didn't even ask to see their passports.

"Come on!" Max called as the children ran to the platform. They still had to clear the security screening and immigration.

The train was in the last stages of boarding with an announcement for all passengers to make their way there immediately. Clearly more interested in timetables than three children who may or may not have been the right age to travel to Paris unaccompanied, the fellow at the immigration counter rushed them through and bid them a good journey.

The children scrambled onto the train and made their way through the car to their allocated seats, only daring to breathe once they were safely on board.

Max fiddled with his watch and sent Kensy a message in Morse code.

Autumn leaned forward in her seat. "Has she replied?"

"Not yet. Unless she's been studying especially hard on it these past few weeks, Morse code isn't Kensy's strongest suit," Max said with a tight grin.

"It's the worst," Carlos griped. "I always mess it up in my reviews. Hey, what if she made her escape somewhere along the way?"

Autumn shook her head. "Not unless she's Houdini. Those guys put a big fat lock on the outside of the van. They didn't want anyone getting in, and they certainly didn't know someone would be wanting to get out."

"I hope she doesn't need to pee on the way – that could be tricky," Carlos said.

"Trust you to think of that." Autumn rolled her eyes. She turned to Max, who was gazing out the window. "Are you going to call your father or Fitz again?"

The boy bit his lip. "I think we should find Kensy first. What was it that Mr. Richardson said during rehearsals the other day? It's easier to ask forgiveness than permission and, as long as we find Kensy, I don't think we'll get into too much trouble – although I'm sure she'll have a lot of explaining to do."

CHAPTER 22

Meanwhile, Kensy had tried everything she could to pick the lock of the van door, but it seemed to be barricaded by something on the other side. Realizing there was no escape until the thieves opened the doors themselves, she set to work finding out exactly what the fellows were transporting. She was about to pull out her phone when she remembered, having read about it just last night, that their use was strictly forbidden on missions and, while this certainly hadn't started out as one, she was fairly certain her grandmother would classify it as such now.

Instead she used her watch to work out where they were. They'd just reached the motorway and were heading south, near the tunnel. At least the road was fairly smooth and straight, and whoever was driving was being careful. Kensy then illuminated the small space with the light on her watch. There were various things — a lamp, a grandfather clock, a table, several jewelry boxes — one that bore the inscription Van Cleef & Arpels and contained a stunning diamond cuff and another housed a dragonfly made entirely of emeralds. It had to be worth a fortune. But there were some other more unusual pieces too — a potted bonsai; a zebra head, which totally gave her the creeps; and a ghoulish mask with horns. It took a few seconds for Kensy to realize exactly what she was looking at. They were the Mesolithic horns that had been stolen from the British Museum!

Kensy sat back, her mind awhirl. She couldn't understand why Theo Richardson would get himself mixed up in all this. While his acting career was on the skids, he was a

Pharos agent first and foremost. He'd taken an oath of allegiance – to protect the greater good and uphold the values of the organization, just as they all had. It didn't make any sense.

Kensy closed her eyes and rested her head in her hands. They were still hours away from Paris. In the darkness, and with the steady thrum of the engine as her lullaby, Kensy started to nod off. A second later, her watch vibrated. She snapped to attention, grateful she'd actually remembered to wear it today.

The message was short and sweet. *We're coming*. It had to be Max, and he was clearly being considerate of her Morse code skills. Kensy smiled and allowed herself to surrender to the pull of sleep. Backup was on the way.

CHAPTER 23

—·· ·· ···· — · ·—· — ··· ·· ——— —·
— ·— —·—· — ·· —·—· ···

Carlos groaned and tossed aside the newspaper someone had left on the opposite seat. He'd never been much good at French. He wished they'd brought something to do – long train rides were so dull – but at least he couldn't complain that his life was boring anymore. This had to be one of the most exciting things he'd ever done.

"So what's the deal with those missing journalists?" Autumn asked.

As the train sped through the tunnel beneath the English Channel, Max filled her and Carlos in on what he knew so far.

"That's awful!" Autumn exclaimed in hushed whispers, trying not to attract the attention of the passengers around them. Carlos listened, wide-eyed.

"But there's been no ransom," Max finished, shaking his head.

Autumn paused, thinking about what she'd seen in the file. "There might be. I saw a number – a really big number – scribbled on one of the pages."

This was news to Max. Surely he hadn't missed it, but with everything going on, it was possible. A ransom could only be a good thing. At least the kidnappers must have made contact.

Carlos's stomach growled and he realized it was almost dinnertime. "Do you want to go and find something to eat?" he asked the others.

"Uh-oh, here comes trouble," Autumn whispered.

Max followed her gaze and Carlos leaned around to see the uniformed ticket inspector making her way through the train.

"But we've got tickets," Max said. "And passports."

"Yeah, and no parents," Carlos reminded him. "We're all still eleven and you're only allowed to travel without an adult once you're twelve. When she checks our passports, she's going to realize and they'll have the gendarmes waiting for us at the other end."

"Okay, let's get some food," Autumn said.

The three children hurried along to the dining car and ordered ham-and-cheese toasties and hot chocolates. The counter jutted out like a little box and there was a table hidden around the back, where they sat to eat.

Autumn watched Carlos with a mixture of fascination and revulsion. He had managed to finish his meal when she'd only taken a few bites. "Slow down, Carlos, or you'll choke," she said, and instantly regretted it. She hoped Max didn't think she sounded like a schoolteacher.

"I'm starving," Carlos protested, standing up. "I'm going to get a hot dog too."

He wasn't gone for more than twenty seconds before he returned, looking worried. "Have you got a plan B? The inspector's coming this way."

Autumn turned to Max. "Is there anything we could use in that backpack of yours?"

The boy rummaged around and pulled out two glass vials with built-in atomizers. One was pale blue and the other amber-colored. Each had a pretty botanical label. "This one makes you laugh uncontrollably and this one makes you smell really bad."

Autumn took the one on the left and walked around to the front of the counter to order another hot chocolate. As she did, she unleashed a spray of laughing liquid into the air.

"What was that?" said the girl at the counter. She felt her cheeks and began to giggle. "That will be two pounds," she said, chuckling to herself.

Autumn smiled and handed the girl some change, then hurried back to her friends, who'd stayed put around the corner. "It works," she said gleefully.

The inspector entered the car. "I could murder a cup of tea," she said with a sigh.

"Murder a cup of tea! Why would you do

that?" The girl giggled. "You're the funniest person I know, Myra."

"I could murder you some days," the woman replied bluntly, "especially when you forget to set aside a donut for me."

The girl began to laugh uncontrollably. Then the woman called Myra did too.

"Excuse me," a man said. "I was wondering if someone could go and clean the lavatory. The one I just went into was disgraceful – there was something on the seat."

The inspector giggled with delight. "Attention, passengers," she said, pretending to speak into a microphone, "we have a Code Brown in the lavatory. I repeat, a Code Brown."

The man's face pinched with indignation. "Madam, I don't know what you think is so funny. It's a disgrace and I will be writing a letter to Eurostar."

The two women were now howling with laughter and attracting a good deal of attention.

"We have to get out of here before we catch it as well," Max said.

"Catch it?!" Autumn glared at him. "You

forgot to mention that bit."

The man who had complained about the bathroom stalked off back toward his seat, although, by the time he sat down, he was chortling to himself.

Another woman entered the car. "Excuse me," she said, and approached the inspector, who was still sniggering like a schoolgirl, "I'm afraid my little boy has been sick on the seat. Do you have something I could clean it up with?"

The woman snorted. "Sick on the seat! That's hilarious."

The girl at the counter was laughing so hard there were tears rolling down her cheeks. Carlos snorted. They really couldn't stay there any longer or they'd be in danger of losing it too.

Autumn donned a blonde wig while Max pulled on a black beanie. Carlos wound a scarf around his neck, partly covering his mouth so that he didn't breathe in any of the fumes. The children emerged from their hiding spot and hurried around the side of the counter.

As they walked past the inspector, she turned and looked at them. "Have I checked your tickets?" she hiccupped.

Autumn nodded. Carlos's nerves got the best of him and he let out a loud rip of wind.

"Did you just pop off?" the woman roared, clutching her sides.

Carlos's face was the color of an overripe tomato and he wanted to sink through the floor.

"He farted!" The inspector pointed at him, then let one rip herself. "We could start our own brass band down here. Anyone else want to contribute?" She could barely speak for laughing.

Autumn tittered, then clamped her hands over her mouth. "Uh-oh, time to go," she mumbled.

The children hurried back to their seats and no one bothered them for the rest of the journey.

CHAPTER 24

The train pulled into Gare du Nord just after quarter past eight. The children hopped off quickly and hurried down the platform toward one of the exits. Suddenly, none of this seemed like a very good idea at all.

"What if we can't find Kensy?" Max said. "What if they take her somewhere different to the address you heard?"

"We're here now – we can't just get back on the train and go home. Kensy needs us," Autumn said. "And if I'm right about *The Hand of God*, then we know what they're planning to steal tonight. If the gang is caught in the act, we'll have blown them apart. Kensy can claim that she was on to them and that's why she helped – or she could just tell the truth and see what your grandmother says."

It was Carlos who spotted something – or rather *someone*. "Come with me – quickly," he said. The urgency in his voice told them there wasn't time for questions. Without a word, Autumn and Max followed him to an alcove where they were hidden from view.

"What is it?" Max whispered.

"Look." Carlos pointed into the crowd of passengers walking down the platform.

"Mr. Richardson! Do you think he followed us?" Max said.

Autumn shrugged. "Remember he told whoever he was talking to on the phone that he was coming to see his daughter tonight? He didn't say where, so she must be close by."

Once the ticket inspector had been taken care of, Autumn had relayed what she'd heard Mr. Richardson saying on the phone as they were leaving the theater. None of them had any idea he had a daughter.

Max looked at his watch. "Kensy won't arrive for at least another two hours — and that's if those guys drive straight here. We might as well follow Mr. Richardson and see where he goes. I mean, he was the one who had Kensy steal the goods, so he's in the thick of all this anyway. He might lead us to the mastermind — or maybe he *is* the mastermind."

The children moved through the crowd, edging ever closer to the man. At one point he turned around and all three of them did too, hoping against hope that he hadn't spotted them.

"We need to split up. We're too obvious together," Carlos said. "Let's meet up outside the entrance."

"We might lose him," Autumn said, and she was worried that they might lose each other as well.

"Just keep sight of him and make sure he doesn't see you," Max said. He gave Autumn a reassuring smile. For a fleeting moment, she allowed herself to appreciate the fact that she was here in Paris with Max – how romantic.

Carlos was right about them separating. They had much more chance of being spotted together, especially as Theo was looking around constantly, as if he suspected someone was tailing him. At one point he stared right at Autumn, who had snatched a cap from a sleeping boy and jammed it on her head, then lowered her face to look like a moody teenager.

Max borrowed a beanie from a rack outside a newsagency and a scarf that had been draped on the back of a woman's chair. His spine tingled when Mr. Richardson stopped and he almost ran straight into the back of him, but the man didn't seem to have a clue it was him. Max couldn't help thinking Mr. Richardson would have been impressed with their artful quick changes.

The children regrouped in time to see Theo hail a taxi and climb into the back seat. Autumn dashed to the curb to flag down the one behind it, but the driver ignored her and drove on. Carlos and Max tried their luck, but it soon became apparent that the taxis were snubbing them deliberately.

Carlos grunted in frustration. "We're going to lose him."

"Come on, I've got an idea," Max said, and raced along the street after Theo's taxi. Fortunately, the evening traffic was heavy and they could still see the vehicle's taillights up ahead. Max stopped at a bank of Vespas lined up in a parking bay.

"This one," Autumn said, running to a pink scooter. It was the vehicle most closely resembling the machine they'd been practicing on downstairs last week. She whipped out her hair clip and unscrewed the light from the front of the bike. "Sorry, Vespa owner, we need this more than you do."

Max dug around in his backpack and pulled out his Pharos-issue Swiss Army knife, from which he retrieved a length of copper wire. He passed it to Autumn, who held it for a few seconds before counting the red, green and black wires and deciding where she needed to put everything.

Carlos leaned in to examine her handiwork. "Are you sure that's how it goes? I thought the green one went with that one there."

Autumn turned and glared at him. "Don't confuse me, Carlos." She connected the wires, then jumped on the machine and gave it a kick start. It faltered. "Darn it!" The girl reexamined the wiring, but it all seemed to be in order.

"Hurry, we've got to get out of here before someone notices what we're doing," Carlos said nervously.

A man walked past, eyeing them curiously. Autumn and Max pretended that it was their bike, with Max complaining loudly that it was broken again while Carlos shielded them from view. Autumn kicked it over for a second time. Miraculously, it sputtered to life.

"Woo-hoo!" Autumn pumped a fist into the air. "Mrs. V.B. would be proud!"

The three of them piled on.

"*Voleur!*" a man shouted. "Get back 'ere!"

But there was no stopping the girl now. The scooter lurched into gear and Autumn twisted the throttle, winding her way through the stationary traffic. "Where did the taxi go?" she called, scanning the roadway.

Max poked his head under Autumn's arm and pointed to the left. "There they are!" His words were barely audible above the noise of beeping horns and angry motorists.

Autumn revved the engine and the boys clung on as she took off. Once they cleared the main intersection, the traffic thinned and was moving freely. She wished the little pink beast had a faster top speed. It would only take one set of red traffic lights and there would be no chance of finding Theo again.

"Look out!" Carlos called as a truck turned a corner into their path.

Without a moment's hesitation, Autumn veered up onto the sidewalk, weaving through pedestrians while shouting at them to get out of the way. Carlos squeezed his eyes shut.

"Get back on the road!" Max yelled.

Autumn did as he bid, jumping off the gutter and onto the street. Carlos almost fell off and only just managed to right himself in time. The wail of a police siren could be heard not far behind them. Carlos turned and saw the Peugeot swing out of a side street. It was racing toward them, lights flashing and sirens blaring.

"Where's the taxi gone?" Max yelled.

"There!" Carlos shouted, and Autumn followed it past rows of elegant storefronts housing all the prestige fashion labels.

They rounded the back of Palais Garnier, its gilt copper statues shining under the streetlights, and reached Place de la Concorde. As they crossed the Champs-Élysées, Max felt a rush of excitement at the realization that they weren't far from the Arc de Triomphe. While he and Kensy had never been to Paris before, their mother had taught them much about the capital over the years and he'd recently taken to studying the atlas she'd gifted him every night to calm his nerves over the impending Pharos review. Max's heart skipped a beat. "The Eiffel Tower!" he gasped. But there was no time to play tourist. They raced over Pont Alexandre III toward Les Invalides, where

Napoleon was buried. The taxi continued through cobblestone streets lined with ornate town houses and elegant storefronts, past leafy parks and towering churches until it came to a stop opposite a primary school.

Autumn hung back, as Esmerelda had taught them to do in such situations, and pulled in behind a row of parked cars. Theo Richardson hopped out of the taxi and stood on the pavement before a residence that was completely shielded from view by a high stone fence. There was a cast-iron gate at the far end, which afforded the children a glimpse of a roofline set quite a way back from the road. It appeared somewhat out of place among the other buildings, which fronted directly onto the sidewalk.

"Look!" Carlos pointed up at the cameras on the top of the pillars. One swiveled in their direction and the children ducked down to hide their faces.

"Whoever lives there wants to guard their privacy, that's for sure," Max said. He stole a peek from around a car tire as Autumn lifted the Vespa onto its stand. Theo spoke into the intercom and was promptly buzzed through the gate.

"Now what?" Carlos said.

"Seeing as we can't get in without being seen, we need to familiarize ourselves with the area. Did anyone see a street sign?" Autumn asked.

"This is Rue las Cases," Max said.

"Have you been memorizing maps again?" Carlos said, raising an eyebrow.

Max grinned. "Guilty."

"That's the address the men said they were coming to." Autumn nodded. "But there's no driveway or access for a car. There must be something around the back."

"It must be on Rue St Dominique," Max said.

The children decided to get a feel for their surroundings. They left the scooter and walked toward Saint Clotilde, a towering neo-Gothic basilica with twin spires, when Max felt his phone vibrate in his pocket. He took it out and stared at the screen. "It's Dad," he said and swallowed hard. "He's going to be so mad — and worried."

"You tried to call him before," Carlos reasoned. "It's not your fault all the adults were busy – we had to come and rescue Kensy."

Max let it ring out, then listened to the voice mail message. A frown appeared on his brow. "That's weird," he said, hanging up. "Granny said that Song left a message for Fitz to pick us up, but he mustn't have gotten it because Dad just left a message saying that he's pursuing a lead tonight with Fitz and Peter, and that he's left a message with Song to take care of us. I'm glad Mum's in Durham with no idea of what's going on because, honestly, the right hand doesn't know what the left hand is doing in our family tonight."

"I mean, it could be a good thing. If we play our cards right, we'll be home before anyone realizes we're gone," Autumn said. "And if we take down the ring of thieves, imagine how happy they'll all be then."

"Let's just find Kensy first and then we can think about what comes next," Carlos said.

Autumn and Max nodded soberly. He was absolutely right.

CHAPTER 25

━━━━━━━━━━━━━━━

▪━▪ ▪ ▪━▪▪ ━━▪ ━▪ ━▪ ▪━ ▪━ ▪ ▪▪▪ ▪▪▪ ▪━ ━▪ ━▪━▪ ▪

Max, Carlos and Autumn walked through
the park and turned left into Rue St
Dominique. A row of surveillance cameras
soon helped them pinpoint the building they
were looking for.

"Keep your heads down and don't stop
until we're all the way past," Max instructed.

They scampered along the road and crouched
behind the parked car, cataloging the number
of cameras that were visible, keeping in mind
that there were likely more that weren't obvious.
Max unzipped his backpack and took out

Kensy's remote-controlled bee. He hadn't ever used it himself as Kensy was very protective of her inventions, but given she wasn't there and they needed to find out more about that building and its occupants, he figured she wouldn't mind.

"Do you know how that works?" Autumn asked.

Max turned it over in his hands, trying to find the "on" switch. "Not exactly, but it can't be too hard to work out, right?"

"You're braver than me," Carlos said with a grin. "Kensy's going to kill you."

Max put on the special glasses and earphones and took out the remote, then, after a few missteps, sent the creature soaring into the air. Except that it almost hit the stone wall and then slammed straight into a window. He eventually managed to regain control and propel it up over the gables.

"What can you see?" Carlos whispered.

Max scanned the grounds greedily. "There are cameras on the roof and there's a large courtyard on the other side of the building.

The house is big – really big – and there are some lights on. There's an open window. I'm going in. Wish me luck – this could get ugly."

The creature flitted into an empty sitting room. He hovered the bee as high as possible to get a proper view. It was elaborately furnished with antiques and curiosities. Nothing terribly interesting caught the eye, although a man dressed in a black suit was stationed at the end of the hall. Max flew the bee through an open doorway and into a large modern kitchen, which was completely at odds with the rest of the decor.

The transmitter in his ear crackled with static and there was a screech of feedback. "Ouch!" Max exclaimed, and pulled out the earpiece. He shook his head before screwing it back in, then continued on a few feet before noticing two figures by the island. He needed to get close so the bee's audio system could pick up what they were saying. Max had to get this landing right or they would miss a perfect opportunity. He hovered the bee, then gently landed it on a cupboard, hopefully high enough that no one would try to take a swipe.

"What's happening?" Autumn asked.

Max frowned and fiddled with the remote. "Mr. Richardson's there. He's sitting in the kitchen and there's a woman . . . but I can only see her back."

"What about the baby?" Carlos said.

Max shook his head. "No sign."

"Have you got another earpiece?" Autumn rummaged through Max's backpack and found the second pair of glasses and earphones. "Perfect!"

Voices crackled through the line. "Is she here? Or have you spirited her away to the countryside again just to spite me?" Theo demanded.

The woman walked around to the other side of the table, her face obscured from view. "First, we have work to do. You can see her after we're done."

"But I'm her father! If we get caught, we'll both go to prison and then what? Who'll look after her?" Theo cradled his head in his hands.

"For once, think about someone other than yourself."

"So he *is* part of the gang of thieves," Autumn gasped.

"And it sounds like he's doing it for his daughter," Max added. "The woman must be blackmailing him. But I still don't get why he wouldn't go to Granny for help."

"Maybe she's made threats against the child," Carlos suggested. "My parents have always said that, if someone tried to harm me, they'd do whatever was necessary to make sure I was okay."

Autumn nodded to herself. "Mr. Richardson could have dug himself a hole so deep he can't see a way out of it."

Max hushed the pair of them. The woman had begun talking again.

"There's a job tonight – our biggest one yet and, now that you're here, you'd better make yourself useful," she said with a hint of amusement.

Theo sat back, defeated. "What is it this time?"

"One of our best customers has requested *The Hand of God*. He has the perfect place for it in his study and we're going to get it for him. At least you and the team are, as soon as those imbeciles get here."

Theo laughed. "You can't be serious. The security will be insane. There's no way we're getting anyone in and out of there without being caught. A job like this takes months of research and training. I can't do anything with those two oafs. They're more of a liability than any help to me."

The woman stroked his cheek tenderly. "Oh, darling Theo, you're so naïve. We have someone on the inside. All you need to do is pick up the loot and deliver it."

Max inched the bee closer to take a better look at the woman. She must have heard the faint buzzing, because she turned and looked straight at Max.

"Victoria De la Vega!" he exclaimed.

"Where did you come from?" The woman's eyes narrowed. She snatched a newspaper from the counter and hastily rolled it up then took a swipe. But Max was faster. The bee took off and sailed right into her face.

Max winced. "Oops."

The woman took another swing and this time she connected with the tiny creature, sending it hurtling through the air.

"That woman – it's Victoria De la Vega!" Max said as he tried to direct the bee toward the ceiling, out of reach.

"She was at the book launch we went to earlier in the week with Granny," Max said. That meant nothing to Carlos, and Autumn didn't know her name either. "She's an actress and the most beautiful woman I've ever seen."

Autumn flinched. "Really? The most beautiful woman you've ever seen?"

There was a metallic crunch and a crack before the line went silent. The camera footage projected on the insides of their glasses fizzled out.

"Uh-oh." Autumn took off her glasses. "She's killed the bee, hasn't she?"

Max grimaced. "Kensy's been working on Ferdinand for ages. I need to get him back."

"What if they discover it's not real and then come looking for us?" Carlos said.

Max shook his head. "I have to go in."

The children looked along the road at the cameras, which pivoted every time there was a movement. Their sensors spared nothing and no one, not even a falling leaf. Just as Max began to wonder how on earth he was going to get past them, a black van pulled into the street, its lights shining behind them. The children dived in front of the green Citroën that was providing their cover.

Autumn checked her watch, then poked her head around. "It's them — it's the van Kensy's trapped inside," she whispered.

In the middle of the stone wall, a pair of oval gates slowly opened.

Max grabbed his backpack and pulled the straps over his shoulders. "Time to move." He sprinted out into the street, shielded from the cameras by the bulk of the black vehicle. Max jumped up onto the small step that protruded from its bumper bar and clung to one of the door handles. Autumn and Carlos did the same and within a few seconds they were through the gates and into the courtyard. As the van came to an abrupt halt, the children thudded against the back doors, but, thankfully, the noise of the motor was enough to hide it.

"What now?" Carlos mouthed.

Max pointed down and they all slipped under the vehicle, just in time to hear the front doors open and see the men's feet hit the ground.

Max was on his watch, sending Kensy a message. The girl's wrist vibrated and she smiled to herself when she realized where they were.

One man was complaining long and loud about a sore backside. As he crunched across the gravel toward the building, they could see him rubbing it.

"Aren't they going to open the van?" Carlos hissed.

"Did you spot those three cameras inside the courtyard too?" Autumn asked Max.

The boy nodded. "Stay here. I'm going out," he said, banking on the fact the van was still out of view.

Max lay on his back and wriggled past

the exhaust pipe, then looked up. By his calculations, the camera that was pointed toward them was angled over the top of the vehicle. If he stayed low, it wouldn't see him. He pushed himself out and examined the padlock on the van then pulled the pin from his Swiss Army knife. He was about to insert it into the mechanism when he heard a door open followed by a shout.

Max retreated beneath the van and watched the feet getting closer and closer until they stopped within a few inches of his face. He held his breath. Autumn and Carlos did too.

The man undid the lock and the chain fell to the ground then he opened the doors. He was muttering to himself about having to unpack the van on his own and called out to his partner to hurry up. They made several trips back and forth to the house.

"There can't be very much left," Autumn said, running through a mental inventory of the objects and remembering that Kensy had hidden behind some furniture. They'd already seen the thieves carry a small table inside.

Max was just about to send Kensy another message to hurry up and get out when the girl's face appeared in front of them. She was lying on her stomach, her head hanging down to peer under the vehicle. She grinned. "Aren't you lot a sight for sore eyes," she said, and dropped down to join them.

If he could have, Max would've hugged his sister for all he was worth, but there simply wasn't room. Autumn was feeling the same way – about both twins.

"I had to tell them," Autumn said. "Sorry."

Kensy shook her head, smiling. "I'm glad you did," she whispered. "Not sure I could handle this on my own."

But there wasn't time to catch up. The men were back for another trip. One was nagging the other to get moving – apparently, they were due at the pickup in twenty minutes. This was news to Kensy. The men hefted and heaved and grunted before trudging away with a grandfather clock and moaning about its weight and who on earth would want one of these old curmudgeonly pieces anyway.

They clearly didn't know it had once belonged to the last Tsar of Russia and was worth a fortune.

"We need to get out of here," Max said. "Or we'll be toast when they move the van and we're left lying on the driveway."

The children agreed and decided to make a dash for the garden, where they could hide in the bushes and work out what to do next. Autumn was first out, followed by Carlos. The pair sped across the gravel, barely making a sound, and hid behind a huge rhododendron bush. Kensy was next. Max was poised to make a run for it when the men reappeared. The boy ducked back under the van. The men were arguing when one slammed the back doors and the other jumped into the driver's seat.

"Where are the keys?" he exclaimed. He couldn't remember taking them out of the ignition. He yelled at the other fellow to fetch them from inside, but the man needed the bathroom badly. They both jumped back out and hurried into the mansion.

Max pushed himself up and threw the keys onto the driver's seat, then sprinted into the garden to join the others.

"That was close," Carlos said.

"What now?" Autumn asked. "We have to get out of here."

Max looked to an upper-floor window. "I need to get the bee."

"What are you talking about?" Kensy glared at him. "Did you do something to Ferdinand?"

Max shrugged. "I didn't mean to, and you can't talk – you're the reason we're in this predicament in the first place."

Kensy wrinkled her lip. Sadly, her brother was right.

Carlos pulled off his black beanie and scratched his head. "We need to catch them in the act and call the authorities."

"I'm so sorry," Kensy said. "This is all my fault. I should have listened to my gut, which said Mr. Richardson was a phony. Why would he want to help me? Obviously, he was only helping himself."

"Stop it, Kens," Max said. "It's fine. I'm

just glad you're all right. Even though you drive me mad some days, I don't know what I'd do without you – although, as payback, I *am* going to beat you in the review."

"Do you know what they're planning to hit?" Kensy asked, and Autumn nodded. "Well, what are we going to do about it?"

Max grinned. "Time for plan B, and we'd better hurry."

CHAPTER 26

▬▬▪ ▪▬▪▬▪▪ ▪▬ ▬▪ ▬▪▪▪

Max and Autumn held their breaths as the van roared into life. They'd managed to sneak inside the vehicle just before the men reappeared.

"Hold on," Max whispered as the van spun around the circular driveway then made a left turn out onto the road.

"I suspect we won't be going far – if they're after what we think they are," Autumn said.

It was mere minutes before the van came to a stop and its front doors squeaked open. This time there were no voices as the men walked away, their footsteps silent on the dewy ground. Autumn and Max waited a few minutes before slipping outside. They were in a dark street, not exactly where Autumn thought they would be, but then driving up to the front entrance wouldn't have been especially smart. Under a canopy of trees and the cover of darkness, the children located the gate, which the men had propped open with a rock.

"Is this where you thought they were going?" Max whispered.

Autumn nodded.

The pair watched through night-vision glasses as the men entered the museum via a side door.

Max couldn't help thinking that all the statues dotted through the garden looked a little creepy in the dark. There were tall pencil pines and a sweep of lawn as well.

"So now what?" the boy asked.

"We wait," Autumn said, hunkering down and making herself comfortable. "Hopefully, they're delivering it back to Victoria's place.

We need to corral them there with this and all the other loot and then we call the police."

But they didn't count on the security guard, who was patrolling the grounds. Things were about to get interesting.

* * *

Back at Rue St Dominique, Carlos and Kensy were plotting the retrieval of Kensy's bee as well as making sure that none of the key players fled the scene. It was curious that Theo hadn't left with the men, as it signaled that their plans must have changed.

The pair was still crouched behind the rhododendron bush when they heard a strange chipping sound, as if someone was picking away at a brick wall.

"We need to get closer to the house," Kensy whispered. She pulled out her hair clip to retrieve three tiny pellets, then fired each of them at the cameras. The pellets opened mid-flight into pancake-sized pieces of fabric, which each found their mark.

298

"Good one," Carlos said admiringly. "I'd never have thought of that."

"Let's just pray it works," the girl said.

The children tiptoed across the gravel. Kensy checked the door the men had been using, but it was locked and, upon closer inspection, it wasn't a mechanism that was easy to pick. There had to be another way in. They continued along the length of the house, keeping low under the windowsills. The building turned a right angle down a side wing, and it was then Carlos spotted a beam of light. It must have been coming from a cellar as it was shining upward. He pointed to it, and the pair began to search for a vent. The chipping noise was getting louder too.

"It's coming from down there," Kensy whispered, and the two headed for the end of the building. Carlos stopped when he saw a glint of metal push through a tiny crack. He and Kensy looked at one another. The girl lay on her stomach and whispered as loudly as she could. "Who's there?" There was no response. "Hello?" Kensy whispered again. "Is anyone down there?"

"Who are you?" a woman replied.

"You tell us your name first," Carlos insisted.

"Trelise," the woman said.

Kensy's eyes widened. "She's one of the missing journalists," she whispered to Carlos. "Why is Theo kidnapping Granny's employees?" Kensy turned back to the vent. "It's Kensy Grey – I met you on Monday night at the launch. Are you okay?"

"I'm not hurt, if that's what you mean, just woozy. And I don't know where I am or why I'm here," Trelise rasped. "I must have upset some very bad people."

"Don't worry, I have a friend with me and we're going to get you out of there as soon as we can. We have a plan," Kensy said. That was overstating the fact, but she wanted to give the woman some confidence that they knew what they were doing.

"I don't think so, sweetheart," a gruff voice snarled as she was snatched from behind.

Before Carlos had time to do anything, a hairy paw covered his mouth and scooped him up too. Kensy kicked and fought, striking the fellow in the stomach. Her foot glanced off as if it was made of steel.

"Let me go!" she screamed.

Her captor clamped his hand over her mouth and, although she tried to bite him, she couldn't get any purchase. The second fellow already had a gag on Carlos and had bound the boy's hands with cable ties. "You're a feisty little princess," the man said, before he too gagged the girl and tied her hands. "And as for you in the basement, we'll be there shortly."

Kensy could barely breathe. The man picked her up as if she was a feather and carried her inside.

CHAPTER 27

.- --.. .. .- -- . --- ..-.
... - .. - ..- . ...

It was Max who spotted the guard first. He was carrying a flashlight and strolling along the path in a uniform with a peaked cap.

"Autumn!" he whispered.

She spun around, but it was too late. The man gave a shout and ran toward them.

The children sped into the darkness with the fellow after them.

"This way." Max took Autumn's hand and the pair charged through the side door, where the men had entered the museum. Inside, silhouettes of statues dotted the room. They could hear the guard's footsteps.

"*Arrêtez!*" he called.

Max spotted an empty plinth and leapt on top, where he assumed the position of The Thinker. Autumn glued herself to the back of a life-sized sculpture of a woman, trying to make herself invisible against the cold stone.

"Where are you, you brats? I will find you and then you will be toast!" the man threatened. He was creeping about, turning this way and that.

Max leapt down and ran past Autumn, grabbing her hand once again. They sped into the next gallery.

"Show yourselves," the man yelled from the next room, smacking his silver flashlight against his hand and swearing at the dead battery.

"Over here." Autumn pulled Max in behind a statue of a man.

"Come out now!" the man demanded.

But Autumn and Max had no intention of revealing themselves to him, unlike all of the naked statues dotted around the place.

"Through here," Max said, and he and Autumn took off again.

Despite huffing and puffing and sounding as if he might keel over at any second, the guard did not give up. He ran back through the room and turned around at the end. This time the children were caught out in the open. Max pulled Autumn onto another plinth then wrapped his arms around her.

"What are you doing?" she whispered.

"Hug me and make it look like you really want to," the boy hissed.

Autumn closed her eyes and could feel Max's breath on her cheek. Her heart was beating so fast she was surprised he couldn't feel it. The man ran past them and Max went to release her, but somehow his lips grazed her cheek. They both felt the spark that neither of them was quite ready for.

"Um, sorry," Max mumbled, but Autumn wasn't in the least. She was in heaven.

Just as the pair caught their breath, the fellow turned around and charged back into the room. Unfortunately, his flashlight was working again too.

"The police are on their way!" he yelled.

Over the next few minutes, the three of them played what amounted to a game of chase around Rodin's masterpieces – in and out of the statues, over the top and around before Autumn led them to the next gallery. They could hear the guard cursing and panting. Thankfully, he was slow, and by the time he reached the room, the children were hidden among *The Burghers of Calais* – or a replica of the original, which was outside in the garden.

As had happened before, he ran straight past them.

"He's either blind or new – surely anyone who's worked here a while would remember what the statues look like." Max grinned as the pair headed for the door.

"Do you think he's in on it?" Autumn asked.

They didn't have to wait long to find out. Minutes later, the men from the van stumbled through the side door. Max and Autumn were hidden nearby, behind a pencil pine.

"I swear there were two children running around in 'ere," complained the security guard, who was leading the way with his flashlight.

"Where are they now?" one man said, mopping his brow with a handkerchief. "You are probably seeing things – although you do not see much, do you, Claude?"

"They ran out the door," the security guard insisted. "They 'ad better be gone – I do not feel like looking for them all night, and I can 'ardly call the police with you two 'ere. You better 'urry up – there is only two minutes before the alarms and cameras are set to come back on and you do know that by tomorrow this will be all over the news. I 'ope you are planning to 'ave it out of the country before then."

"We are taking it to 'er then she will give us final instructions," the other man replied.

Autumn and Max waited until the men

were loading the van before they made their move. They sprinted out through the gate and into the night.

"There they are!" the security guard called.

"Be quiet, you imbecile," the first man hissed. "Go after them for all I care, but if you do not lock up soon, we will all be locked up for a very long time."

The man exhaled and did as he was bid. Besides, he had no desire to chase two children along the streets of Paris.

CHAPTER 28

—·—· ——— —·· ··—· · ··· ··—· ·· —— · ——— —·· ···

Kensy wriggled on the stone floor, straining against her bonds. There was a musty smell in the air and all she could see was darkness, courtesy of her blindfold. She wasn't sure where Carlos had been taken, although she had a sense there was a warm body close by. She'd heard a few strange grunts and hoped it was Carlos and not some oversized rottweiler ready to chew her face off if she managed to get free.

Kensy wet the gag in her mouth to the point that the fabric stretched enough for her to finally spit it out just as she heard the slide of a bolt and the creak of a door. There was an audible gasp as the person stepped into the room. She heard the door close and footsteps approach.

"What on earth are you doing here?" a familiar voice whispered, before pulling off her blindfold.

Kensy blinked and found herself staring straight at Theo Richardson. There was an old bed in the room with a bare mattress and a small sink in the corner. Carlos was sitting a few feet away and there wasn't a rabid guard dog in sight. Theo whipped the blindfold and gag from the boy as well.

"You are too kind, dear sir," Carlos mumbled.

Theo frowned at him. It was hardly the time for Shakespeare, although he couldn't help thinking his life had come to resemble one of the man's great tragedies.

"You set me up," Kensy rasped. "Why did I ever believe that you wanted to help me? You just used me – and I did a really good job, stealing all those things and not getting caught. I should be getting a cut of the action."

Carlos snorted. Trust Kensy to say something like that.

The handsome actor looked like a naughty schoolboy. "I never meant to involve you," he protested. "Well, not to this extent. I was left with no choice. I needed someone who was capable and you wanted the extra help with your studies . . ."

Kensy's face hardened. "Oh, no you don't. Don't try to blame me for what you've done. I was just an innocent latecomer."

"And why have you kidnapped three journalists from the *Beacon*?" Carlos added.

Theo's forehead puckered. "I don't know what you're talking about," he said. From the look of horror on his face, it seemed likely he was telling the truth.

"Trelise Fulton-Jennings is here and I'd hazard a guess that so are Harry Stokes and Jamila Assad. Those two have been missing for over a week with no ransom note — try explaining that to Granny next time you see her." Kensy's green eyes narrowed. "Are you a double agent? Who are you working for?"

"Actually, I think there is a ransom," Carlos said. "Autumn saw something written in a file at your house." He turned to Theo. "By the way, demanding half a billion dollars? That's obscene. No one needs that much money."

Kensy was surprised by this revelation. "I suppose you plan to kill them if you don't get the cash."

Theo shook his head vigorously. "I don't know what you're talking about with the journalists. Trelise is a friend – I'd *never* hurt her. And I never meant for any of this to happen. I've been a fool and now I'm in too deep. I still don't understand why you're here, but you need to know that you're in far greater danger now than you were back in London."

Kensy quickly explained what had happened at the theater, how she'd ended up in the van and how the others had followed her to Paris.

"We were on the same train as you," Carlos said. "And you didn't see us even when we were right behind you on the platform."

Theo groaned. "Oh my goodness, that

train journey was the worst. This crazy ticket inspector kept on cackling like a psychotic chicken. When she realized who I was, she tried to get me to kiss her!"

Carlos grinned, thinking it served the man right.

Theo paced around the room, his footsteps echoing. He turned and faced the children. "If what you say is true, she's more of a monster than I ever realized."

"Who is she?" Kensy asked. There hadn't been time for the others to explain before Max and Autumn had to leave in the van.

"Some actress," Carlos said. "Max recognized her from that book launch you went to."

Kensy gasped. Surely not. "Victoria De la Vega?" she exclaimed, eyeballing Theo. "I knew you were lying when you said you'd never met her. I saw her talking to you from her car . . . So are you the father of her baby then?"

Theo nodded miserably, the anguish clear on his face. Kensy was slightly taken aback – that had been a long shot. "That's the only reason I'm involved in all this," he said. "Victoria has been blackmailing me, telling me that if I didn't do as she asked, I'd never see Sophie again."

"Oh," Kensy said, almost feeling sorry for him.

Theo's phone beeped in his pocket. He pulled it out and checked the screen. "I need to get back upstairs."

"So whose side are you on then?" Kensy challenged. "Are you one of us or are you with her?"

Theo looked at the girl, an ache in his eyes. "I'm with my daughter. If I don't do Victoria's dirty work, I'm going to lose Sophie and I don't doubt what that evil woman is capable of now."

"We can help you, sir," Carlos said. "Because if you get caught – and believe me, you will – you'll have no way out and you'll go to prison. Even Dame Spencer can't fix everything."

Theo took a deep breath. "All right," he said finally. "There's not much time, so tell me your plan and make it quick."

"Untie us first," Kensy said. "Then we'll talk."

CHAPTER 29

—————————

```
.—. ——— —.—. —.— ——..——
.——. .— .——. . .— . ——..——
... —.—. .. ... ... ——— .—. ...
```

M_{ax} and Autumn reached the town house just in time to see the gates closing after the van. They had to find another way inside. Max tried Kensy's watch, but there was no response.

Autumn's brow puckered with worry. "Do you think something's happened to them?"

Max frowned. "There's only one way to find out. Let's get in from the other side, but we'll need to avoid the cameras."

"I don't see how – they're everywhere," Autumn said, biting her lip.

The children ran around to Rue las Cases.

"We can get in from there." Max pointed at the building next door. "The roof."

Autumn swallowed hard when she realized there had to be over a hundred feet between them. While her parkour skills had been improving, she didn't think she could make it that far, even with the longest run-up.

Max squeezed her arm. "Don't worry, I've got a zip line – as long as we can shoot it far enough and secure the cable, it will hold our weight and we can enter from above. Thankfully, that apartment building is higher than the mansion and, as long as they're not monitoring the sky as well, we'll be fine."

Autumn breathed a small sigh of relief, although the idea of shooting through the air and across the garden below was not without its concerns.

The security at the apartment building turned out to be on the lesser side of secure as it took mere minutes for the pair to get to the roof. Max pulled out what looked like a tiny tape measure. The hardest part was finding a target to anchor it, but Max used his magnifying glasses to assess the situation before sending the cable shooting into the air. It pierced the masonry on the roof at the far end. He wrapped the other end around one of the chimneys nearby.

Max didn't know if he should go first or send Autumn.

"I'll go," they said in unison, and grinned at one another. "You go," they said at exactly the same time again, then laughed nervously.

"Max, I'm scared," Autumn said suddenly.

"Me too," he replied. Max took her hand. "We can do this. We might not be fully up to the task, but we have to try. I can hear Song in my head – Confucius says that he who hesitates is lost . . . but I don't actually think Confucius said that because I'm pretty sure it's just a saying that lots of people use, and maybe it was a proverb in the *Bible*."

Autumn giggled. "I love Song," she said, though not as much as she loved Max. Maybe one day she'd be able to tell him.

"I think there's only one scientific way to decide which one of us goes first," Max said. "Three rounds of rock, paper, scissors?"

CHAPTER 30

"*Put* this in the guard's drink," Kensy said, passing Theo one of the vials from her bag. "It's called *Sleeping Beauty*. If it works properly, the recipient will be out for hours – although Grand-mère and Grand-père said it wasn't quite perfect yet and sometimes it's had the opposite effect. Let's hope that doesn't happen this time around."

The man nodded and looked at his watch. "I really must go. I have a feeling Victoria has a getaway plan and I'm not part of it."

"Stall her," Kensy said. "Keep her upstairs, and when those creeps come back with the loot, get them inside too. We'll leave the journalists where they are until it's over. None of them are Pharos."

Theo could hardly believe he was taking orders from an eleven-year-old, but her plan was a good one. He had nothing. Ever since he'd fallen for Victoria, his entire life had been shrouded in a haze of love – that was, until she recruited him to her gang and he realized that the life of luxury she lived – apparently on the earnings from her film career – was a total lie. The woman had invested heavily in a string of failed businesses that she was desperate to hide from the public, so she'd changed tack. It had all started one night when she was invited to a party at a mansion in Mayfair. The host, a buffoon of a man called Pierre, had spent the night showing off his art collection and bragging shamelessly about the money he'd spent. Another guest had commented while they were being shown around the house how much he would have loved that Matisse on his own wall. It had started as innocently as that.

Weeks later, Victoria hatched a plan to steal the painting for him. The man was so impressed that he told some friends who then told some other friends and so the word had spread. Before she knew it, Victoria was making millions procuring rare pieces for clients all over the world. Today was her most ambitious heist yet, having moved on from private collections to the British Museum and the Rodin Gallery, from which *The Hand of God* was currently on its way back to the house – to be driven to the border and put on a plane. Theo had fast fallen out of love with Victoria, but he couldn't leave his daughter. She was everything to him.

The children waited until they heard a thud. They opened the door and tiptoed into the hallway to find their guard snoozing on the table. Carlos relieved the man of his keys and quickly tied him up, then he and Kensy hurried to the end of the hall. They wanted to be sure Trelise was okay, but they'd leave her exactly where she was for now – the last thing they needed was a journalist asking questions about what they were doing there.

"Trelise?" Kensy called through one of the locked doors.

"I'm here," the woman rasped. "Can you let me out?"

"Soon, I promise," Kensy replied. "Just sit tight. We won't be long."

* * *

Meanwhile, Theo had done a great job of spiking several more drinks. Victoria's battalion of bodyguards were now snoring all over the house, although she was yet to realize it.

The woman spun around from the window as Theo entered the room. "What took you so long?" she demanded. "What was the story with those children in the garden?"

"Just local kids playing a game. We let them go home – they were so scared I doubt we'll ever see them again," he said smoothly. "I brought you a drink." He passed it to her, but she set it down on a side table.

The delivery men appeared in the doorway.

"You took your time," she cooed. "Do you have it?"

The pair nodded.

"Right. Theo, you take the Mercedes with the Rodin in the trunk. The delivery instructions are all here, and please don't mess it up," Victoria said, passing him an envelope. She leaned in close, batting her eyelashes. "You know I'm relying on you."

"What are you doing?" he asked.

"I'm going out of town for a few days," she said.

An older woman appeared at the other end of the room, carrying a toddler in her arms.

"Sophie!" Theo cried, and took the child from her. The baby began to cry. "Sweetheart, I'm sorry. Daddy's missed you so much." He kissed the child's forehead.

"Give her back to Zelda, Theo. You've upset her," Victoria said, her voice brittle like a sheet of ice.

"She's my daughter," the man said. "I have every right to see her. Please, Victoria, I've done everything you've asked."

As Zelda reached for the child, the baby wriggled toward her, arms outstretched. She took Sophie and walked away.

"You'll see her again soon, but first . . ." Victoria motioned toward the open door.

To the woman's surprise, Kensy and Carlos stepped around from the hallway, blocking her path. "You're not going anywhere," Kensy said, eyeballing the woman. Her beauty was undeniable and very distracting.

Victoria arched an eyebrow. "Who are you? And, more importantly, how did you get into *my* house?" She gestured to the thieves. "Basil, Remy, do something!" But one fellow was slumped in a chair. The other hadn't made it that far. He'd toppled face-first onto the ground and was out cold.

"It's over," Kensy said. "We know you've been blackmailing Mr. Richardson to work for you and your dirty ring of thieves."

Victoria threw her head back and laughed, her long tresses shimmering. "How ridiculous. You, child, have a vivid imagination."

"Don't play dumb with me," Kensy retorted.

She didn't appreciate being condescended to. "You're not acting now, Victoria – not that you were ever very good at it anyway."

"How dare you!" Victoria spun around and raced away. In the blink of an eye, she disappeared behind the curtains.

Carlos and Kensy chased after her, but when they pulled back the fabric, she was gone.

"There's a panel – she's in the wall," Kensy said.

"This must be one of the houses that was used to hide fugitives in the war," Carlos said. "It will be riddled with secret passageways."

Kensy looked at the boy curiously.

"We studied it in history," Carlos said with a shrug. "Sometimes I do pay attention, you know."

"And you can give the baby back too," Theo said, prying the child from Zelda's arms.

As the old woman fled for the door, Carlos whipped out a lasso shoelace and flung it across the room. It snapped around her ankles and she crashed to the ground.

"Come on," Kensy said. "We can't let

Victoria get away." She ran her hands over the panel and located the mechanism. Before she and Carlos disappeared into the tunnel, she turned back to Theo, who was cradling his child in his arms. "Call Granny. She'll know who to send."

Seconds later, Kensy and Carlos were scampering along in the cold, dark cavity that appeared to run at least half the length of the house. Kensy shone a flashlight around, but there was no sign of Victoria. Although they couldn't see her, they could hear her footsteps.

"This way," Kensy shouted, her voice echoing around them. The pair took off, but the place was like an ant nest with tunnels in every direction. "We have to split up!"

Up on the roof, Autumn and Max were searching for a way into the house when a hatch opened and Victoria flew out.

The woman spotted them and rolled her eyes. "Seriously, there are more of you?"

A helicopter swooped into view. Its shadow blocked the crescent moon as it descended toward them, its rotors whumping.

Autumn thought for a moment. She pulled out the photograph she'd taken from the file at Ponsonby Terrace. "You're her . . . You're as beautiful as Max said you were."

"Victoria! Stop!" Max commanded.

A rope ladder tumbled from the sky, hitting the roof.

"Oh, no you don't, lady!" Autumn charged at the woman, sending her flying, but the girl hadn't counted on Victoria being quite so tough.

Despite her elegance, Victoria was no shrinking violet. She clambered to her feet and ran back toward the ladder. This time Max was on it. He grabbed the woman as she climbed the first few rungs. Victoria kicked at the boy's head, connecting with his cheek.

"Ow!" Max shouted, but he wasn't going to lose her now. The chopper began to lift further into the sky. Max shimmied up as quickly as he could.

"Max!" Autumn screamed from below. "Let go!"

But the boy was determined. He grabbed

Victoria by the ankle, then reached around into his back pocket for a tiny device Kensy had given him before he and Autumn had gone to the museum. "This had better work, Kens," he muttered as he pressed it against the woman's bare skin. She began to shake violently and relinquished her hold of the rope ladder, falling backward. Except her foot was caught and she was dangling like a fish in a net.

Kensy and Carlos emerged from the hatch in the roof, having used the noise of the helicopter as their guide.

"Grab her!" Max called, and the children scrambled to untangle the woman.

A bullet from a gunman above whizzed past Max's ear, followed by another and another. The children pulled Victoria free just as another helicopter thundered toward them. The rope ladder began to rise and the first aircraft disappeared into the night sky, toward the Eiffel Tower.

Victoria fell hard onto the roof. Carlos and Kensy grabbed her arms. She struggled for a while before calming down but the children didn't dare let go.

"Has anyone got a spare shoelace we can tie her up with?" Kensy called.

A light from the second chopper illuminated the rooftop and the children shielded their eyes. A black JetRanger hovered above them. Kensy squinted and realized that this time they weren't in any danger of being shot at.

"Fitz! Dad!" Max shouted.

Peter Petrovska was with them too. The chopper descended low enough for the three men to jump from its open doors. The momentary distraction provided Victoria with the chance she'd been waiting for. With all her strength, she tossed Carlos and Kensy away like rag dolls, then ran to the edge of the roof and, in one almighty jump, leapt toward the chopper skids, grabbing the rail with both hands. The aircraft spun around, trying to shake her off, but to no avail.

Kensy crouched down to pull a tiny poison-laced ninja star from an insert in the sole of her shoe, then waited until the chopper steadied. The girl lined up her target, then aimed and threw. Seconds later, Victoria lost consciousness and dropped like a stone onto the rooftop. This time they took no chances. Carlos bound her wrists and ankles.

Fitz and Ed looked at one another. "Well, that was impressive," Fitz said.

Kensy ran into her father's embrace. "I'm sorry, Dad. I'm so sorry."

Ed shook his head. "Darling, you have nothing to be sorry for. By the sounds of it, you kids have just cracked a huge case, although I'm sure you're aware you'll get no thanks for it outside the organization."

"But I was so silly," she said miserably.

"We all make mistakes, sweetheart." Ed grinned. "Sometimes it's better to learn the hard way – you'll never make the same error again."

Kensy looked up at her dad and smiled. He pulled Max into his embrace too.

"Are the journalists here?" Peter asked.

Kensy nodded.

"I'll take you to them," Carlos offered.

"And I'll call the French Secret Service to

clean things up here," Fitz said.

"What will happen to Mr. Richardson?" Max asked his father.

"Your grandmother will deal with him and, don't worry, he's confessed to everything. Poor fellow has made some terrible choices, but your grandmother won't see him separated from the baby – she obviously means the world to him." He gave Kensy's shoulders a squeeze. "Kids are like that."

Kensy rested her head on her father's arm. "I love you, Dad."

"I love you guys too, and if I was in Theo's position, I would have done the same thing."

"No, you wouldn't," Kensy said. "Because Mum would never have made you choose."

A look passed between the two of them. Kensy's eyes widened as she realized that was exactly what her mother had done all those years ago, when they first disappeared to start a new, anonymous life. Her father had chosen her mother and the twins over Pharos and his own mother. That must have been the hardest decision he'd ever made.

"Come on, let's go home," Ed said.

The twins liked the sound of that. London was really beginning to feel as if it was where they belonged.

"And perhaps we won't tell your mum about all this until she returns from Durham," Ed said. "She needs to concentrate on her exams."

"Good idea, Dad," Max said with a grin.

CHAPTER 31

— · ··· — ·· —· ——· — ·· —— · ···

Kensy closed her notebook and stared at the cover. She had done everything she could and now it was just a matter of remembering what she'd studied. There was a knock and Max opened her bedroom door. He was dressed and ready for school.

"How are you feeling?" he asked, leaning against the door frame.

Kensy shrugged, swiveling from side to side in her chair. "Okay, I think."

"You know, whatever happens today, we can only do our best," Max said, offering her a smile.

"Yeah, I know," she replied. "I just hope it's good enough for Granny. She still hasn't said anything to me about what happened – do you think she's really mad?"

Max shook his head.

"Are you mad at me?" she asked, picking at a thread on her sweater.

"No, of course not," Max said kindly, stepping into the room. "I'm just glad that you're okay and everything worked out."

Kensy smiled sheepishly. "I'm sorry I kept a secret from you. It was vain and silly and that's not us, is it?"

Max swallowed the lump of guilt in his throat. He still hadn't told her about Magoo's note and it was eating away at him. It wasn't because he didn't want to. It was just that, despite decoding another two words, he still didn't know if it meant anything. There was no point upsetting her if the whole thing proved to be his own overactive imagination, and especially now, right before their review.

The twins had gone to school on Monday morning as if nothing had happened the night before. Victoria De la Vega was locked up in a Paris prison, awaiting extradition to London, and news of her exploits were splashed across the front pages of every paper in the United Kingdom and Europe. The woman was painted as a mastermind, and now MI6 and Scotland Yard were working to locate the missing items and have them returned to their rightful owners. Of course, the recipients of the ill-gotten goods claimed they had no idea their purchases were stolen – although Jamila, Harry and Trelise were determined to get to the bottom of that too.

It turned out that the journalists had been kidnapped because they'd all gotten dangerously close to the trail in different ways. Jamila had been on to Victoria's string of failed businesses, while Harry had been on the verge of blowing the theft ring wide open. It was Trelise who had worked out that Theo and Victoria had had a child together. She had innocently congratulated the woman on her baby at the party in the hopes of getting an exclusive, and the next thing she knew she woke up in a dank cellar in Paris.

"Has Dad told Mum yet?" Kensy asked.

Max shook his head. "He said we'll tell her together when she gets back tonight. But I think we should tone it down, Kens. She worries a lot, you know."

Kensy grimaced. For now they needed to get to school. Their review was scheduled to start at half past eight.

"Breakfast!" Fitz's voice floated up the stairs, along with the smell of freshly made pancakes.

They both gazed in the direction of the kitchen, neither of them making a move. "I'm not especially hungry, but we'd better eat otherwise Fitz will think we've gone off his cooking," Max said.

"Song is definitely better, which is a total bummer because it sounds like Granny needs him at Alexandria for a while." Kensy sighed. "I was looking forward to a rematch in the dojo."

Their father had wished them luck before he left for work and their mother had telephoned too. She was looking forward to getting home.

Breakfast was a silent affair. The children gathered their bags and Fitz escorted them to school. He gave them a hug and said they'd be fine. As Kensy and Max made their way through the school reception, jangling with nerves, they were surprised to see Mr. Richardson standing in the hallway. He hadn't been at school the day before and the twins had wondered if he'd be back.

"Hiya, kids!" he called out a little too enthusiastically. "Don't forget we have a rehearsal after school today."

Blair happened to be walking past. "Good to know," she said sarcastically. "What happened to yesterday? I mean, my drama teacher in Sydney always told us that you need to be in prison or on your deathbed to get out of rehearsals this close to a show."

The twins grinned at Theo, who bit his lip.

"Looking forward to it, sir," Max said.

"Break a leg," Theo whispered, then made a face. "Sorry, bad choice of words. Go get 'em."

Kensy laughed. "We know what you mean. Thanks, sir. You okay?"

"Better than ever," he replied cheerfully. "I might be spending quite a bit of time here – like, the rest of my life. It's definitely a more attractive proposition than the alternative of a posting in Siberia."

"What about Sophie?" Max asked.

Theo's face lit up at the mention of his daughter. "She's at home with my parents. Thank you for everything. If it wasn't for you two, I don't know what would have happened."

Kensy and Max smiled. "You're not off the hook yet, sir," Kensy said. "You'd better find me a really good job for the rest of the production – I'm not sorting props. I think I've done enough of that already. I want to be on lighting or sound or something that requires me to use my brain, which, I might add, is pretty impressive."

Theo smiled, wondering who he would have to displace to get Kensy just the right role.

"We'd better get moving," Max said, fingering the note in his pocket. He'd have to forget about the puzzle for now and concentrate on whatever was thrown at them downstairs, but he'd work it out eventually. He had to. *Future, imminent* and *threat*. What it all meant was anyone's guess, but he had a feeling he and his sister's lives might depend on him working out the rest of it – and soon.

MORSE CODE

Developed by Samuel F. B. Morse, an inventor of the telegraph, Morse code is a system of communication that uses a series of dots and dashes to relay messages. It was designed with efficiency in mind, as the length of each symbol is approximately inverse to the rate of occurrence in text of the English character it represents. For example, "E," the most commonly used letter of the English alphabet, has the shortest code – a single dot. In an emergency, Morse code can be generated by improvised methods, such as turning a light on and off, tapping an object, or sounding a horn or whistle, making it one of the simplest and most versatile methods of telecommunication. In fact, the most common internationally recognized distress signal is SOS — three dots followed by three dashes and then three dots.

... --- ...

While learning Morse code is not easy, it can be done in much the same way as one learns a new language. You can give it a go by using the cipher on the next page to decode the chapter headings in this book and see if you can tap them out for your friends to work out too.

A	.—		O	———
B	—...		P	.——.
C	—.—.		Q	——.—
D	—..		R	.—.
E	.		S	...
F	..—.		T	—
G	——.		U	..—
H	....		V	...—
I	..		W	.——
J	.———		X	—..—
K	—.—		Y	—.——
L	.—..		Z	——..
M	——		,	——..——
N	—.		?	..——..

ABOUT
THE AUTHOR

Jacqueline Harvey taught for many years in girls' boarding schools. She is the author of the bestselling Alice-Miranda series and the Clementine Rose series, and was awarded Honor Book in the 2006 Australian CBC Awards for her picture book *The Sound of the Sea*. She now writes full time and is working on more Alice-Miranda, Clementine Rose, and Kensy and Max adventures.

jacquelineharvey.com.au

Read Them All!